"But...Mitch." Georgie sighs with contentment. "So. Hot."

"Uh, so ewww. He's a pig."

"I'm not defending his bewildering ways, but I saw the two of you at the party."

"So?" I seriously don't know what she's getting at.

"So...there were sparks lighting up that corner of the room where you two were making out."

"Those weren't sparks. They were warning flares from the universe. I just couldn't see them because I was blinded by Mitch's male-superiority complex. Did you know it glows neon green in the dark?"

"What glows?"

"His complex. It's so toxic that it's like some radioactive leprosy that eats away at the female brain. It's how he gets so many women to sleep with him."

She laughs. "Oh, so now he's a disease?"

"I'm lucky to be alive," I say as a matter of fact.

"While I couldn't be more grateful that my best friend wasn't turned into a phosphorescent sex doll by this well-endowed monster of epic hotness, I think she might be overvilifying the man. Just a tad."

"Bite your tongue." I hang my damp towel on the little hook next to the door. I like my things neat and organized, which is why when my mom redid my room a few years ago, she added an entire wall of white storage c

"I'm being serious, Abi. Sam is an excellent judge of character, and I doubt he'd be friends with Mitch if he were that rotten of a human being."

But Sam didn't defend Mitch when I brought the issue up. In fact, he confirmed that Mitch has a thing against female bodyguards. In other words, Sam knows Mitch isn't an angel.

"All I'm saying," she adds, "is that I think there's more to the story."

I slide on a black lace thong. "He's a turdler, so if you believe otherwise, then there's something you're not telling me."

PRAISE FOR THE OHELLNO SERIES

"With a smoldering cover that gives us just a hint as to one of the surprises in store for readers, *Digging a Hole* was an unputdownable rollicking good time of a romance that captured my heart immediately."

—Sara, Harlequin Junkies

"What I love about this book is what I love about most of the books that I have read by this author. It is the witty banter, the snarky comments and the connection between the two main characters."

—Three Chicks and Their Books, on *SMART TASS*

"I seriously LOVE Mimi Jean Pamfiloff's talented writing style so much that I can add her to my addiction list."

—Jennifer Person, The Power of Three Readers, on *SMART TASS*

"Where does she come up with some of this stuff?!? Mimi's mind must be a fantastic place. Filled with blood thirsty unicorns and now, warrior squirrels and naked yoga cults, I stand in awe of her imagination. Her stories are funny and twisty and filled with enough crazy sexiness that I can't put them down. I couldn't have anticipated where *Digging A Hole* was going, but I gladly held on for the ride."

—Leigh, Guilty Pleasures Book Reviews, on *DIGGING A HOLE*

"Oh, Henry!!! It's sweet, funny, and oh so sexy. A definite FIVE-STAR read that has the three H's: HILARITY, HOTNESS, and HEART. The amazingly talented Ms. Pamfiloff has written your next book boyfriend, Henry Walton. Get ready to fall in love with this cocky unfiltered athlete and his quirky smartass match, Elle! You will love their banter and his quest to win her over."

—Bestselling author of *Until Alex*, J. Nathan

"Digging A Hole is a laugh out loud, fast paced, crazy ride of a romantic comedy."

—Louise's Book Buzz Blog, on *DIGGING A HOLE*

"Mimi Jean Pamfiloff has topped even herself! Wonderful characters, some truly twisted events and some pretty awesome reading as two people learn to work as partners and trust in one another for support!"

—Tome Tender, on *OH HENRY*

"*Oh Henry* ratcheted everything up a notch. Still some sweet romance, some very funny situations, and a little bit of angst as both Elle and Henry are dealing with some serious issues. And, what would a Mimi Jean book be without one of her little added twists."

—Carol's Reviews

"It is funny, entertaining, and an absolute delight"

—As You Wish Reviews, on *DIGGING A HOLE*

OTHER WORKS BY MIMI JEAN PAMFILOFF

COMING SOON!

Colel (Immortal Matchmakers, Book 5) ←It'll bee next. I promise! ☺

The Librarian's Vampire Assistant, Book 3 ←Gah!! What will Miriam say? #IamaVampire

My Pen is Huge (OHellNo, Book 5) ←Oh no, Mimi didn't. (She did.) #NaughtyTitle

The Boyfriend Collector, Part 2 ←Steamy Alert! (Windshield wipers required for your reading glasses.)

THE ACCIDENTALLY YOURS SERIES

(Paranormal Romance/Humor)

Accidentally in Love with…a God? (Book 1) ←My very first book baby ((hugs)).

Accidentally Married to…a Vampire? (Book 2)

Sun God Seeks…Surrogate? (Book 3)

Accidentally…Evil? (a Novella) (Book 3.5)

Vampires Need Not…Apply? (Book 4)

Accidentally…Cimil? (a Novella) (Book 4.5) ←Evil unicorn explained.

Accidentally…Over? (Series Finale) (Book 5)

THE FATE BOOK SERIES

(Standalones/New Adult Suspense/Humor)

Fate Book ←Careful what you wish for!

Fate Book Two ←Ditto.

THE FUGLY SERIES

(Standalones/Contemporary Romance)

Fugly ←Still makes me cry.

it's a fugly life

THE HAPPY PANTS SERIES

(Standalones/Romantic Comedy)

The Happy Pants Café (Prequel)

Tailored for Trouble (Book 1)

Leather Pants (Book 2)

Skinny Pants (Book 3) ←Probably the last nookie cookie book. ((Sad face.))

IMMORTAL MATCHMAKERS, INC., SERIES

(Standalones/Paranormal/Humor)

The Immortal Matchmakers (Book 1)

Tommaso (Book 2)

God of Wine (Book 3) ←My fave cover ever! Slurrrrp.

The Goddess of Forgetfulness (Book 4)

THE KING SERIES

(Dark Fantasy)

King's (Book 1) ←EVIL

King for a Day (Book 2)

King of Me (Book 3) ←Not so evil?

Mack (Book 4)

Ten Club (Series Finale, Book 5) ←Not telling.

THE LIBRARIAN'S VAMPIRE ASSISTANT

(Mystery/Humor)

The Librarian's Vampire Assistant (Book 1)

The Librarian's Vampire Assistant (Book 2) ←Mr. Nice wants more Fanged Love!

THE MERMEN TRILOGY

(Dark Fantasy)

Mermen (Part 1)

MerMadmen (Part 2)

MerCiless (Part 3) ←Crazy Dirt Will NEVER Die!!!

MR. ROOK'S ISLAND SERIES

(Romantic Suspense)

Mr. Rook (Part 1)

Pawn (Part 2)

Check (Part 3, Finale) ←Luke is no longer speaking to me. Wants own book.

THE OHELLNO SERIES

(Standalones/New Adult/Romantic Comedy)

Smart Tass (Book 1)

Oh Henry (Book 2)

Digging A Hole (Book 3)

Battle of the Bulge (OHellNo, Book 4) ←You are here. ☺

BATTLE OF THE BULGE

THE OHELLNO SERIES
BOOK 4

MIMI JEAN PAMFILOFF

A Mimi Boutique Novel

Cover Design by Earthly Charms
Developmental Editing by Latoya Smith
Copyediting and Proof Reading by Pauline Nolet
Formatting by Paul Salvette

DEDICATION

To foot rubs and the brave men who dare to touch our stinky feet after a hard day.

BATTLE OF THE BULGE

CHAPTER ONE

ABI

If you could pick one word to describe yourself, what would it be?

Optimist?

Extrovert?

Driven or feisty?

If you'd asked me a few years ago, I would have said shy. Seriously, turtles had nothin' on me. I was the girl in school who always pushed her hair down around her face, sat in the back of the classroom, and rarely raised her hand. I never would've described myself as brave. Or deadly.

Of course, I'm all grown up now, nearly twenty-two, and I can't afford to be that girl anymore. Especially because I need money. A lot of it. Which is why I'm standing in the slushy mud after hiking seven hours in the freezing Alaskan snow while carrying a fifty-pound pack filled with survival gear. This is the world's toughest job interview, but if I pass, I'll make three times what I could anywhere else.

A projectile whizzes past my ear, and I plunge headfirst into a thick pile of snow between two towering pines. *Jesus! Who am I kidding?* I'm no GI Abi! I'm a certified geekoid. President of the *Star Trek* Uhura Club, avid romance-book lover, cowbell player in my university's beginners' band, and the founder of Business is Sexy enthusiast group who promotes business and finance majors among the women's clubs on campus. All these groups are new endeavors for me—my way of trying to be more social—so I can learn to love new things.

Okay. Most new things. This bodyguard bootcamp? Possibly a huge mistake.

Of course, I'm not naïve. I know that life rarely turns out the way people expect. When my father died of a heart attack about six years ago, I never imagined how much I'd miss him. Suddenly, this man who used to drive me crazy with his lectures about grabbing the bull by the horns became the one person no man could ever compare to. Losing him made me see how special he was and how lucky we were to have him—something my mother knew for years.

After he died, her life began falling apart. Not because she wallowed or felt sorry for herself. Not even. She is a pillar of strength, both as a human being and as the owner of an interior design company. Her misfortunes have all been a series of random events—some horrible client who spent one hundred K on custom furniture and design work then decided to sue for his money back because his new girlfriend didn't like the style. That same week, there was a flood in her warehouse and her insurance company went under. Fabrics, curtains, pillows, and her entire house-staging inventory for the realtor clients. Gone. It's been one disaster after another, but she still manages to keep a high chin and a wide smile.

Honestly, her can-do attitude is what inspired me to apply for a job as a bodyguard. I'm fighting for a chance to get our mortgage back to square, pay for my final semester of college, and keep her interior design business from tanking. If I'm lucky, I'll run my own business someday, too.

I remove my dirty white parka, toss it to the snow-covered ground, and press my back to a wide tree trunk. I'm frozen to the bone, but my camo thermal shirt will blend in better with the bark.

One more kill, Abi. Just one more, and this will all be over. No, I'm not really going to kill anyone. But I do have to tag one more trainer with my airsoft rifle. Otherwise, I fail bootcamp. I'm all out of ammo, so after this last pellet, it's game over.

"You got this, girl," I whisper to myself, ignoring the aches in my back, legs, and arms from crouching and crawling over rocks and frozen branches.

I hear my target's soft footsteps crunching through the freshly fallen snow. *This is it. Steady. Keep calm*...I wrap my frozen pink finger around the trigger and hold my breath. *You got this, Abi. You got this.*

Suddenly, I hear more footsteps approaching to my left. And to my right! They've been tracking me all day, and now I'm surrounded.

Just like I'd hoped. Because sometimes life hands you lemons. And other times it hands you grenades.

I smile, reach into my pocket, and grab my pellet bomb. *Abi's graduating today, boys!*

CHAPTER TWO

Houston, Texas. Thirty-six hours later.

"Keep the change." Eager to see my mom, I shove sixty bucks at the cabdriver, grab my black duffel bag, and push open the car door. I haven't been home for over four weeks, but it feels like a lifetime ago. She thinks I've been off training for a sales job at some extreme camping-gear company, which will explain why my skin is chapped from the cold and my long brown hair has lost five inches. Who knew you could literally give yourself a trim by freezing the hell out of your hair and just snapping the strands like twigs? Anyway, good intentions or not, I hate lying to her, but we need the money.

I stand in the driveway, and a gust of cool Tex-an air hits my face. Compared to where I've been, this feels like the freakin' tropics. Plus, there's something about Houston in February that brings back sweet memories of anticipation, when you know flip-flops, bathing suits, and spring break are just around the corner.

Errr...you'll be working. Remember? No spring break for you. My best friend, Georgie Walton, is going to be crushed. We always go to the beach in early April because we're inseparable. The funny thing about us, though, is that we couldn't be more different, aside from growing up as two shy nerds. She always liked sweats; I like heels and skirts. She grew up in a wealthy family with security guards and servants, always running away from the limelight and her demanding parents. *A full-blown introvert.* I, on the other hand, grew up very middle-class with two loving parents, always wishing I were brave enough to stand tall in front of a room full of people. *A wannabe extrovert.*

This last year, though, we've both been stepping out of our comfort zones and taking charge.

Shy girls no more! Cue theme to *Superman.*

No. Wait. Make that *Wonder Woman.*

Okay, yes. I maaay still struggle from time to time with finding my voice, but that doesn't mean I'm weak or don't have opinions. I just tend to clam up when my emotions run high, almost like I kinda don't trust myself.

Calm mind equals rational words.

Flustered mind equals embarrassing gobbledygook.

With duffel bag in hand, I take the walkway around the side of our yellow ranch-style house since my mom isn't home from work yet and I always lose my key, so I stopped carrying one. I leave it under a rock out back near the hibernating flower garden. In the front of our house there are rosebushes that will blossom soon along with the bulbs in the ground. My mom is a master gardener. I barely get along with a salad.

"Abi!" I hear a deep voice call out.

Without thinking, I drop my bag, reach for my sidearm, and crouch. *Okay, dorkee-doo, you have no sidearm.*

"Nice." Trying his darnedest not to laugh, the infamous Sam McDaniel stands at the edge of my driveway on our quiet residential street. Sam, who's in his early thirties, loves a crisp black suit, which he's wearing today. He's tall, well-built, and a bit terrifying at times. Kind of reminds me of a bulkier, young Clint Eastwood, especially when he uses those stormy gray eyes to give you the stink eye. He's also my best friend, Georgie's fiancé and my new boss.

"Don't laugh." I stand up straight, dusting off my jeans. "Your stupid bootcamp has permanently dented my brain."

He walks up, grabs my duffel bag off the ground, and holds it out. "You say dented, I say well trained and appropriately paranoid for a soon-to-be bodyguard."

I'm about to chew him out for failing to warn me about what I was in for—"*Think of it as a paid Alaskan vacation, Abi. Only, they'll teach you how to use a gun and incapacitate someone three times your size.*" Vacation, my ass. I'll be dreaming of snow in my butt crack for an entire year. I literally had icicles forming inside my woman cave. Okay, it's more of a very tight crevasse, not a cave, but I swear there were crystal formations happening down there, and not due to lack of sex. Though, I haven't had any of that lately.

Or a good orgasm. Not since…not since the man whose name shall not be spoken, whose face will only be remembered as that of a heinous reptilian beast with a slithery tongue. And devil horns. Coming from his chin. Yes, heinous.

Wait. I hit pause on my mental effigy to the Horned One, remembering that my mom will be home any second and Sam is standing in my driveway. If she sees him, she'll absolutely wonder why he's here, and she can't know about my new job. No. Freaking. Way.

A. She'll kill me.

B. She'll keel over.

C. What was the point of having an abominable snow-snatch in my pants for four weeks if we're both dead before I make any money?

Point is, my mom would never approve of my new job. No parent in his or her right mind would want their daughter taking a bullet for a stranger. Not that I intend to, but that's what being a bodyguard essentially boils down to, doesn't it? If you fail at preventing the bullet from leaving the chamber, then that bullet has your name on it.

The good news is that whatever team Sam assigns me to, my role is what he refers to as "the owl" position. Eyes and ears only. I'll be the person who hangs back and blends in. Anything suspicious, I report it to the lead, who's the guy or gal with real training you always see in movies, standing beside the client in full view like a warning sign to anyone who wants to try something. Me, I'm part of the crowd, minding my own business, texting or window-shopping or whatever seems appropriate given the location and the client. Being an owl is low risk for "civilian types" like me, even though I have to be prepared to defend myself or the client in a pinch.

I just hope whoever my client is, she's someone smart who won't needlessly put anyone in harm's way. And I hope she's someone important. A Nobel Prize winner or—*Oh! I know. A scientist who's going to make the first commercially sold male-bot who does your dishes, folds your clothes, and orders your favorite dishes at restaurants so you can say you're not hungry and then eat all his food anyway.* Sadly, no matter how important the client, this job will worry my mother to death. It will make her feel like a failure as a parent if she knows I'm putting my life on the line for money. *For her. For us.*

"Sam, I don't want to seem rude or ungrateful, but you need to go. If my mom sees you, she's going to—"

Sam crosses his ripped arms over his chest, the

fabric of his black blazer stretching to its limits. "You didn't tell your mom about working for me?"

"No." I grab his elbow and pull him to the side of our yard, between two tall hedges bordering the next-door neighbor's property. "And I don't plan to."

He frowns with those cool, silvery eyes.

I won't lie. I used to have a tiny crush on Sam when we met at the pharma company I interned at last year. Believe it or not, he was an FBI agent posing as a sales VP, trying to bust the company's executives for a bunch of dirty business involving black-market cancer drugs 'n stuff. Georgie interned there too, and then she and Sam ended up together. *Lucky.* He was the best thing ever to happen to her, and since she's like a sister to me, Sam now feels more like a big brother rather than an ex-marine, ex-FBI agent, and my new boss. I just hope working for him doesn't cause friction between me and Georgie. She's my best friend.

"Abi, you're going to have enough stress dealing with the job. You don't need to pile on by keeping secrets from your mother. You might need her for support."

I glance at my watch. It's six oh five. *She'll be home any second!*

"It's none of your business, *boss man*, and who are you to lecture me about keeping secrets?" I raise one brow for emphasis.

"I was undercover. That's not the same thing."

"Fine. You got me there, but this is still my personal life, and you can't—"

He grabs my shoulder and squeezes gently. "Georgie is already upset with me for hiring you. The only reason she backed off is because I told her how perfect you are for this role and that you really want it."

I roll my eyes. *That's Georgie for ya.* "Why does she always have to be so supportive and nice?" I grumble petulantly.

"Because she loves you. And she will be all over my ass if she thinks you're not serious. Serious people don't run around and keep their new jobs a secret." He shrugs. "I happen to agree."

"Meaning?"

"If you're not all in, then you're a danger to yourself, the entire team, and the client. You can't work for me."

I don't intend to do this forever, but I do take it seriously. Proof being that I just spent four weeks playing Arctic penguin because my future is riding on the money. I need to finish my last semester of college, and I want to eventually open a nonprofit. Watching my mom struggle after my father's death made me realize how little help there is for mothers who find themselves widowed. One day, your husband is alive and you're both paying the mortgage, making ends meet, and saving money for retirement and your children's future. The next you're alone and facing being homeless with mouths to feed. But if you don't have family to lean on or friends to help you, then you're on your own. Banks won't loan to you. *Too risky.* Mortgage companies don't care. Credit card companies keep sending bills with more and more interest tacked on. There has to be a better way to help these women restructure their finances—low-interest loans, negotiating with lenders, pro bono assistance in selling their homes instead of losing them in foreclosures. Something. They shouldn't have to face the loss of their husbands and their homes too. Once I get that off the ground, I'll extend to widowed fathers.

I take a deep breath. "I am serious about working for you, Sam. And I promise I will tell my mom when the time is right."

"Soon, I hope?"

I nod. "Soon. But you need to go. She's already heard about your new company, and I don't want her putting two and two together."

"I'll leave, but we still need to talk."

"About?"

"About your first client. It's why I came in person."

"Oh no. What's wrong? Who is it?" I hope it's not some scummy, man-whoring musician or some lame-o diva who just wants to look cool and have an entourage.

Sam looks away, that scruffy jaw pulsing with tension. "Be at the office at six."

"In the morning?" I whine.

He slides on his mirrored sunglasses, all seriousness. "Your first job starts tomorrow at seven thirty, but I need to brief you." He glances over his shoulder. "Your mother just came around the corner." He walks off through the neighbor's yard and gets into his black SUV parked at the curb.

A minute later, my mother pulls up in her white van with her Carter Designs logo, a scripted font CD, on the side.

Wait. How did he hear her coming from four blocks away? That man is so mysterious.

"Abi!" My mom, who has long brown hair and light brown eyes—almost a moss green at times, just like mine—flies from her van the moment she spots me. "Baby, your cheeks are all red! And you cut your hair!"

"Thought a tomato face and bob might suit me," I lie.

We hug tightly, and I feel the tension leave her body. "You have no idea how much I missed you. I almost cried every night, worrying."

And this is how she reacts when she thinks I've been somewhere safe. There's no way she can ever find out about my new job. Of course, I can't tell Sam she doesn't know because he'll fire me.

Now I have to deal with this mystery client, too? Jesus. Why do I feel like four weeks in Alaska was just the start of this grueling journey?

CHAPTER THREE

"I'm sorry, but did you just say…did you just say…?" The next morning I'm in Sam's new office—a sterile-looking space with almost no furniture and a big window overlooking the parking lot—feeling my knees knock so hard that I'm about to fall over.

This isn't happening. I plunk down in one of two gray armchairs facing his spotless desk.

"Abi," Sam pumps his palms in the air like an ode to the god of tranquility, encouraging me to keep it together, "I know you have history with Mit—"

"No! You won't speak his name. Not to me. Not ever. The Oh-Slimy-One is never to be mentioned in my presence." I seriously want to cry, which is why I cover my face. "How could you do this?"

"Abi." Sam's computer chair creaks as he gets up. A moment later I feel his hand on my shoulder. "You told Georgie that the night with *him* meant nothing. You said you'd forgotten it and couldn't care less."

I drop my hands and shrug. "Yeah, well..." There's no way I'm going to tell my boss what happened. *I should have known better than to believe I meant anything to that...to that degenerate penis hooker. Pooker.* I got played. Plain and simple.

Sam sighs and throws in a throaty grunt. "If I was incorrect in my assumptions about the situation, then I understand if you don't want the job. And I certainly don't want you to take it if you hold animosity toward the client. But the way Mit—"

"No. Do *not* say his name."

Sam raises his large hands in surrender. "From the way our *client* spoke, I got the impression that you were both out to have a little casual fun. Nothing more. Which I completely respect since you're both adults, so no judgment here."

"What?" I snap. "There was nothing *casual* about it, Sam. He literally grabbed my clothes the next morning, threw them at me, and shoved me out the front door!" I had been invited by that horrible man's cousin to that horrible man's housewarming party. Horrible man and I ended up dancing and talking, and when he kissed me, I lost it. *It* being my ability to reason.

How the hell did I let "the Bulge" sweet-talk me? Seriously, maybe I deserved the humiliating dismissal. I mean, the only reason I wanted to sleep with Oh-Nameless-Scummy-One is because he's hot. So, so hot. And because he's known for being...well,

well endowed.

But don't get the wrong impression. I'm not that woman. Shallow. One-nighters. Wanting a man for his meat instead of his brains. But Mitch Hofer had looked so sexy with that tall, rock-hard swimmer's body and unkempt light brown hair with golden streaks. After all the things he said—tender and real—I decided to throw a little caution to the wind, which is probably why things turned out so damned horrible. *Karma.* We were naked, I was ready, and he was apparently sleepy because Mitch passed out right on top of me. I tried waking him—cheek slapping (the ones on his face), cheek pinching (the ones on his ass), and some vigorous shoulder shaking.

No dice.

No sex either.

I was disappointed, but I figured maybe we could pick up where we left off in the morning. I fell asleep only to be thrown out at the crack of dawn. *What a first-rate asshole! I'm so happy we didn't have sex.*

"Well," Sam says, "like it or not, *he* is the client. An important one. And I've made a commitment to make sure he has around-the-clock security."

Sam's only been in business a little over a month, and I know he needs this contract. For starters, just look at these offices. With all the cameras and security doors, it's got to be costing him a fortune. Not to mention the location is near downtown.

Still, "Why didn't you tell me he was the client?"

"Protocol. No one gets names until they're assigned to a team. But I listened carefully to what you said to Georgie: 'Nothing. He's nothing.' That's what you said, Abi. And when I proposed you come on board, I told you that you might not love the clients, but we don't get paid for that. We get paid to keep them safe. You said yes."

Dammit! Dammit! Dammit! He's right. I was so desperate for money that I failed to consider I might not be working for the savior of humanity.

Sam takes the other gray chair beside me in front of his desk. He looks worried—frown, flat lips, and lots of slow breathing.

Oh no. This is a strong man. Tough. Trained. Dedicated. To see him stressing is the sort of thing that makes an impact.

"What aren't you telling me?" I ask.

He sighs with exasperation. "You're the perfect owl for the job, Abi. You dress right. You talk right. You have balls, but look like a wallflower. You're a Trojan horse in a skirt, which is why I offered you the surveillance position. But if you can't put your life on the line for him, then I can't hire you."

"I need the money, Sam. This isn't just a job—"

"Georgie told me about your situation. She also told me you refuse to take charity, which I respect. But know that if you really need the money, I'll mortgage my house if I have to. I'll help you any way I can. But I can't put Mitch in any more danger than he already is, and that will be the case if you're not all in."

The look in Sam's eyes is so intense that I don't complain about the mention of *his* name.

Sam adds, "My sources at the FBI and CIA confirmed that the threat is real, Abi."

"Can you tell me what kind of threat? I mean, who are these people? Why are they after a swimmer?" *Besides the fact he's a jackass and maybe they want his hide for a nice jackass coat.* There's a market for everything these days. Example: the horrible swimsuits Mr. Jackass wears from his sponsor, Weeno. They have things like panda or elephant faces on the front, positioned just so, in order to make the animal's nose protrude like little penis puppets. *Ick. So wrong.*

"I can't give you specifics about the source of the threat, Abi. I'm sorry."

"That hardly seems fair." I fold my arms over my chest.

"It's not because I don't trust you. Some of the information is classified."

"What about the portion that's not?"

Still seated, Sam rubs his rough chin. "Bottom line, we don't know specifically who's coming after Mitch, and we don't know when. We only know they are coming and they've been given a million dollars to make it happen."

I squint my eyes. "We are talking about Mitch Hofer here, right? Swimsuit model, giant ego, loves paddling around swimming pools all day like a giant man-child?"

Sam shakes his head with disapproval at my comment. "All you need to know and accept is that the danger is very, very real or I wouldn't have taken Mitch as a client. We're not a fashion accessory. Our clients have credible threats. They need genuine security. So if you can't provide it, I'm sorry, but you're off the team."

I crinkle my nose. "No other assignments?"

"Not unless you think you can be an owl for a sumo wrestler in Tokyo or a Russian diplomat who's anti-Putin and in exile in Norway."

I toggle my lips, mulling it over. I can't blend in with a sumo posse—I wouldn't know the first thing about walking around in a kimono with those weird flip-flops—and both locations are much too far away from my mom. With the exception of the last four weeks, we hang out and talk almost every day. Usually over dinner. There was a time when I hated how she forced me to do it, but now I'm glad. She refused to let my angsty teen years drive a wedge between us. She and Georgie are my best friends.

I sigh, thinking about the twenty thousand dollars I need by the end of next month just to stop the bleeding. I get paid nothing for bootcamp since it cost Sam over ten thousand to send me, so if I don't take the job guarding Mitch, my mom and I lose our house, her interior design business goes under, and Sam is out ten K.

Shit. I can't quit on her, and I can't do that to Sam. Not when I know he took a huge leap of faith by hiring me. I have no military training. No background in law enforcement. Nothing. He picked me because he thinks I'm smart and he needs a woman who can look the part. Surveillance is the cornerstone for this kind of work.

"I will..." I swallow down a resentful lump of pride sticking in my throat, "do my part to keep Mitch safe. I promise."

His cool gray eyes are filled with skepticism. "You sure, Abi?"

I nod.

"All right. Because as you're aware, the client travels with an entourage of women." Sam gets up and walks around to the other side of his desk.

"You mean groupies."

"More or less. And it's why I need someone like you. Someone who won't get distracted by Mitch's looks."

"It's your lucky day, because I have zero interest in that man."

"Abi, I'm serious. It's strictly prohibited to get personally involved. To do so is grounds for immediate dismissal. No exceptions."

Exactly which part of my revulsion is he mistaking for the desire to hook up with Mitch again? I get that Sam is afraid if he assigns a woman to Mitch's entourage, she'll end up jumping into bed with him or spend all of her time drooling, but I'd rather give up romance novels for an eternity than hit that.

"You have nothing to worry about, Sam. I need this job. There's no way in hell I'd risk losing it."

"Excellent. Because you'll be accompanying Mitch on photo shoots as well as swim practices and competitions. It's imperative that you're focused on what's around you instead of his swimsuit. Or what's in it."

What Sam means to say is Mitch's "giant shlong." Well, I've already seen it. Sort of. Mitch and I didn't have sex, but we did engage in some very vigorous foreplay. He'd taken his thick cock and rubbed it right over my—

No! I push away the memories of my night with Mitch Hofer. *A generous salami does not make up for his despicable personality.*

I clear my throat. "I repeat, I will not be distracted by the client." Not him. Not his ripped tanned abs or muscular back. Not his bulging swimsuit or those sultry bedroom eyes. *And I definitely won't be distracted by his sex-lips.*

"Then welcome aboard, Abi."

I stand, expecting Sam to shake my hand, but he hands me a case instead. I open it, and inside is a shiny silver gun no bigger than the palm of my hand.

"It's loaded," he adds. "Be careful. And your gear and outfits are with Cray."

Cray. Short for Crazy, I guess? He's Sam's operations manager. Gear, reservations, anything at all, we go to Cray.

"Thanks, Sam." I check to see if the gun's safety is on and slide it into my little over-the-shoulder purse.

"You're sure, Abi?" Sam asks one last time.

"Stop worrying. This is going to work out great."

He shakes his head at the floor and places a hand on his waist. "If anything happened to you, I couldn't live with it."

"Wow. Didn't know you cared so much."

"I meant that Georgie would kill me." He grins.

"Har, har."

Sam's expression turns cold.

"What?" I ask.

"Be careful, Abi. This is the most rewarding job you'll ever have, but it will also be the most challenging. And..."

"Yes?"

"There aren't many people in this world cut out for it. But you are. Even if you're only doing surveillance, it makes me feel better knowing you'll be there. You're smart. You're quick. You know how to make a bad situation turn to your advantage."

I can't help wondering how he's come to this conclusion. Georgie is our common denominator. She must've talked me up.

"Thanks for the vote of confidence," I say and turn for the door.

"Don't mention it. Cray will give you your clothing on the way out. Remember to practice acting extra slutty this morning."

Huh?

Sam chuckles and picks up a call.

"Here you go." Cray, a tall Scottish man with long red hair and muscles like boulders hands me a big shopping bag. "You have five outfits to get you started. There's a membership card for Pistol Whippers. They can get you anything you need disguised in a feminine package—knives, ammo, mace. Everything's made to look like lipstick, a dildo, or perfume."

I stare blankly, wondering what sort of woman would buy a knife disguised as a vibrator. And isn't it usually the other way around? Dildo in a lipstick case or whatever. Not that I'd know. *Much.*

Cray adds, "Just be sure to keep your receipts and submit an expense report to me."

I grip the bag. "Got it."

"And a word of advice: Buy several pairs of sunglasses. They get lost quickly and you'll need them. Hard to keep track of that stuff when you're dodging bullets."

"Bullets?" But I'm supposed to be an owl. I stay back from the client and watch the crowd, watch everything. I mean, yeah, if there's a threat and no one else can handle it, I'm the man. Or wo-man.

Otherwise, I've been trained to never break my cover. Even if there's a situation, I'm supposed to tell our team lead of any threats—like in the case of a hit that's coming from a coordinated group versus just one person.

Hmm...I wonder what this "real" threat is that Sam mentioned. The Oh-Slimy-One probably pissed off the wrong woman. Now she's hunting him and wants his bulge for her trophy wall.

I imagine Mitch and his junk—stuffed, shellacked, and mounted to a piece of wood like a giant swordfish. The plaque would read "Giant Dick," referring to the man, not his member.

I smile and head to the elevator. Suddenly, reality starts sinking in, and I feel a ripple of panic tear through me. I know I'm only an owl, but now it's all starting to feel real. Life-threateningly real. *Ohmygod. I'm a bodyguard.*

CHAPTER FOUR

I can't do this. The snake-headed bastard is forty feet away, doing an interview with a local morning talk show. There are two men with earpieces, wearing black blazers, waiting for Mr. Slimy to exit the set.

My hands start to sweat and tremble. My heart does the whole adrenaline thing. I hope he doesn't make a scene when he sees me. "*I never want to see you again. Get lost. You're nothing to me.*" These are basically the words he spouted through his closed front door the morning after his housewarming party here in Houston. Mitch is originally from Australia. He is also a multi-gold-medal Olympic swimmer and an extremely famous swimsuit model. That man has calendars, a line of body oil, workout videos, and his own brand of protein drinks called Big Meat, "for the man who likes to show and grow."

Uh...yuck much? He's so damned full of himself.

And he almost filled you, too. My mind flashes to a moment of heated kisses, our bodies grinding, the smell of him on my skin, and—

Stop it.

He meant nothing to me. I meant nothing to him. I'm not giving up a job I need for a guy who isn't worth my time. Whatever he has to say, I can handle it. I can stay professional.

I hang back by the exit and spot Sleeze Bucket's chick posse. Unlike me, most are tall blondes. I'm about five five, brown hair, and light brown eyes. I usually like skirts and heels, but what I'm wearing looks like I rolled my ass into bed after a night of clubbing and didn't bother changing. Cheetah-pattern heels, matching micromini skirt, and a hot pink tube top.

And where's my gun? It's next to my phone crammed down my cleavage. Padded bras come in handy for this kind of stuff. My B cups look like full Cs because I've got so much storage going on in there.

I fish out a piece of gum from my titty purse, pop it in my mouth, and throw the wrapper on the floor as my role dictates. No class. Not that anyone's watching me. All eyes are on Gutter Puppy, who's wearing a snug pair of worn jeans and a baby blue oxford, just like the one he wore the night we met. I remember the shirt well because of how it accentuated his beautiful broad shoulders and lean Y-shaped body.

No. No... You're not going there.

Mitch continues talking to Miss Sally Sunshine, the overly peppy host, about his "extremely awesome swimsuit sponsor, geared for the man who's not ashamed of his masculinity like the other loser swimsuits out there."

"Can't believe I have to protect you with my body," I mutter.

The lead bodyguard and technically my direct boss, Phil, turns his head and does a double take from the side of the set. I wiggle my fingers in his direction and chomp hard on my gum, letting it snap a couple of times. "Hey, baby. You want gum? I got gum," I whisper loudly.

Phil gives me a suspicious look, like I can't possibly be that ridiculous.

Oh, but I can... "This grape flavor is yummy. Tastes like Robitussin." That's the code I'm supposed to use so he knows I'm part of his team without making it obvious. Thing is, half the time, threats to clients come from people they know—learned that in training. So I'm like a super mole, inserted to keep an eye on Mitch's friends, manager, and entourage. Like a good little owl, I will listen carefully and watch everyone.

I'm supposed to tell Mitch how much I love grape gum, too, so he knows I'm on his side. Sam's already instructed Mitch to treat me like one of his fuck-pets.

Gag.

The interview concludes, and the studio audience, mostly women, start to roar.

"Have my baby, Mitch!"

"I'll swim naked with you!"

"Show us your bulge, baby!"

I hold back my disgust. If it ever got out what a sleezy pooker he is, women everywhere wouldn't be throwing themselves at him; they'd throw him into a volcano.

I watch Mitch shake hands with the host and take a bow, followed by him blowing kisses to the audience, who's going nutso.

I shimmy down my micromini and straighten my back, summoning my steady nerves. I can't believe I'm this nervous to see him again.

Mitch and his broad shoulders make their way to the edge of the set, and his two big bodyguards take to his sides. Amusingly, Mitch is taller than both men, though his athletic frame is less husky.

The princess posse rushes to Mitch's front. "Ohmygod, Mitch! Like, that was sooo, like, perfect! You look so hawwwt, OMG."

Where did he find these women? The '80s? I put on my game face and strut toward him, ready for anything.

He spots me approaching, and for a split second we lock eyes, which makes my heart do summersaults. The thing is, aside from his fast swimming, Mitch Hofer is known first and foremost for his...well, giant cock. It's hard to miss since he spends most of his time in a tiny swimsuit. Runner-up is his six-pack. The man's stomach looks like a giant tan tortoise shell that's been stretched out over his abs. But third in line for his most noticeable physical trait is his eyes. They're hazel, which is stunning enough on their own, but what makes his so unique are the light green bands around the outside of the irises. He's won *Teen Lust* magazine's sexiest eyes award five years in a row, despite being twenty-six.

Well, he's not getting any prizes from me, so…

I walk toward him and stop just shy of his pack of horny she-hyenas. "Hey, Mitch," I say in my sugariest Texan tone. "I like grape gum."

His charming smile melts away, and he gives me a look, like he's wondering at what age I got kicked in the head by a mule. "Well then, guess you should buy some more," he says, though with his Australian accent, it sounds more like *Wheel, theyne. Guess you should boi summor.*

I often wonder why some Aussies sound like Crocodile Dundee and others like Brits with a twist. Whatever the reason, Mitch is all *Aussie. Or…Eez oil Aussie?* And yeah, he sounds hot. But now I know "bey-ta." I won't ever get sucked in by that face, bod, or sweet accent again.

He puts his arms over two of the groupies' shoulders, and the three flow around me like I'm a river rock of little importance. Heading for the exit, they laugh and nuzzle like they're in some sex club where rubbing noses is the secret handshake.

I can't believe he just blew me off like that. Maybe Sam forgot to tell him I was joining the team? *Or maybe he forgot me.*

I swivel in Mitch's direction, the rage bubbling deep inside my cold chest. It's cold because the temperature in this studio is set to "igloo" and I'm wearing a pink tube sock as a shirt.

"What are you doing?" scowls Phil in my ear, grabbing me by the shoulder but keeping a friendly smile on his lips. Phil is a portly man with a dark mustache and hair.

I look up at him, unsure what he means.

"You're supposed to blend in with Mitch's entourage," he adds through clenched teeth. "Now pretend you're flirting with me so we have a reason to be talking." He pats my ass, and I resist belting him. We went through all this in training. If I'm playing the part of horndog, then I have to embrace the bun, mustard, and frank with a smile. If I'm playing the role of maid, I dust, scrub, and wash. If we're in a crowd, I'm the fan trying to grab a photo for IG, offering my body for the client's love child. Point is, political correctness means nothing when you're trying to prevent someone from having their brains blown out.

I giggle at Phil for the sake of my cover. "You're cute."

He nods. "Thanks, babe," he says loudly. "But Mitch doesn't like waiting for his girls, and we're on a schedule."

Thankfully, I'm only pretending to be one of "his girls." Still, the thought nauseates me. What did

I ever see in this guy?

I scurry out the door to the parking lot. It's a chilly February morning and I'm regretting not wearing a coat. When I catch up to the entourage, the last girl is ducking into the back of the limo. To my surprise, Mitch is being a gentleman and helping the women in.

When he gets to me, he drops his hand and scowls. "Oh, it's grape-gum girl. Who invited you *ageen*?" he asks.

Is he serious? If yes, then this bonehead swimmer is thicker than an iceberg.

Phil appears at my side. "Sir, this is your raffle winner from last week. You know, the one from the radio show? Spend a week with Mitch Hofer."

Mitch's hazel eyes twitch for a moment. "Oh." He looks at me. "Sorree 'bout that, sweetheart."

"No problem." I nod coolly, but I'm imagining pounding my fists into his supple sex-lips.

He seriously doesn't remember me? What a huge dick! It's one thing that he doesn't home in on the whole grape-gum-code thing, but it's another that he has zero reaction to seeing me.

Calm yourself, Abi. This is good. If he really doesn't remember me, then problem solved. *Still, how could he forget that night?*

I slide into the backseat, and the other girls eye me like a wilted piece of lettuce who's come to spoil their delicious gourmet sandwich.

I look straight ahead, unsure of what to say.

Mitch takes the seat next to me, closest to the door, and the animosity from his harem only spikes.

"Home, Mr. Hoffer?" asks the driver.

"Yeah. I'm tired. That morning workout before the show was tough."

"Very good, sir," says the driver as Phil and the other suit get into the vehicle.

"And can you drop the girls off? Wherever they want," Mitch says.

A unanimous "Awww. What?" explodes from the women.

"Sorry, ladies," Mitch says, "but I have a full day. We'll continue the fun some other time."

Phil clears his throat. "Don't you want to keep just one, sir? For your *relaxation*?" He glances at me as if to say, *Hint-hint; grape-gum lady needs to stay.*

Mitch glances at me from the corner of his eyes. "Sure. I'll keep bubblegum girl, here. She looks like she's not too demanding in the heavy conversation department."

What in the…? Did he just call me dumb?

I refrain from showing my true sentiments. I made the honors list at Texas U's School of Business six semesters in a row. I completed a bodyguard training that was so rigorous half the class dropped out in one week. And most were dudes. With military backgrounds! My IQ isn't genius like Georgie's sister-in-law, Elle, but I'm still damned smart.

Just ignore him. I mean, this guy wears a bikini

and swims in glorified puddles for a living.

"Saweet!" I snap my gum. "I'm totally up for fun. Heehee..."

The other girls shoot harpoons with their eyes.

Thirty minutes later, the limo is dropping off the last girl. Apparently, they all live in the dorms or close to the university. From what I've been told, not that I care or anything, Mitch moved to Houston after being enticed to swim for the university's team and train there for the next summer Olympics. I love my university, but it's a little weird to uproot and leave home like he did. He was months away from graduating with his bachelor's in sports management or something, and he just upped and left to start over. So weird.

Mitch says a polite goodbye to the women, but doesn't kiss or hug any of the ladies.

Huh. That's odd. Aren't they his sex kittens or whatever?

Now with the two of us alone in the back of the limo, the air permeates with an unpleasant silence. I know the driver is part of our team and so are Phil and the other suit, so it seems like a good time to ask, "Why am I coming along?" I'm just the team's extra set of eyes.

Phil turns his large body to face me in the back. "Mitch likes to host parties, which means you'll be doing a lot of work there. Get familiar with the layout, entrances, and secure exits. I'll come by later to hear your analysis."

I'm still a trainee, but Sam is a firm believer in learning on the job. He wants us all to be able to assess locations on our own—TV studios, photo-shoot locations, whatever, since the team can't always huddle and do it together. Bodyguarding is a fluid process where you have to be prepared for anything. One minute, you're walking across a parking lot. The next, someone fires a shot and you find yourself scrambling to extract the client and yourself in one piece. You have to be able to assess your surroundings on the fly and find the safest route out.

"Sounds good. What time?" I ask.

"Around six o'clock."

But it's eight in the morning. "I hate to be a pill, but I only need about an hour for the assessment. What do you want me to do with the rest of my time?"

"Do your job and cement yourself in as part of Mitch's entourage," Phil replies. "There are plenty of people watching at his house."

I try not to let my emotions show, because what I think Phil means to say is that Mitch has a staff of four—a driver (one of ours), a personal chef, a housekeeper, and a personal assistant. I'm supposed to convince them and anyone else in his social circle that I'm one of Mitch's girls. No one can suspect I'm part of the detail. *Fine. I signed up for this. I won't complain.*

Mitch leans in and whispers, "Don't worry. I'm

going to take a power nap. You can just admire my manly muscles while I sleep." He chuckles like a cocky SOB. "You're welcome."

I'd rather stare at your dirty underwear. "So generous. Thank you, Mr. Hofer," I whisper back with an overtly sugary tone. "But I have a real job: protecting you and those big strong arms with my little ol' girly body."

Mitch's smug smile takes a nosedive. "As if you could."

"What's that supposed to mean, Mr. Hofer?" I whisper back.

"For the record, you're here against my will." He speaks into my ear.

I blink. "Meaning?"

"A female bodyguard? *Pffi!* Now there's a knee-slapper."

Wow. What a knuckle-dragging, club-thumping caveman. With every passing moment in the Bulge's presence, I'm finding it harder and harder to keep my promise to Sam. If some guy showed up in this very moment shooting arrows at Mitch's head, I'd be the person ducking on the floor, saying, "Get 'em! Get 'em before he procreates!"

My life for Mitch's? Ohellno!

I smile demurely. "Well, my tits can be used as flotation devices in case of a water landing, so don't discount my value entirely."

Mitch glances down at my fake C cups and then turns his head toward the window. "Not even that," he mutters.

I snap my head in his direction. "Uh, sorry?"

He shrugs. "I can see the outline of your gun, grape-gum girl. Next time, try a more discreet hiding place. Better yet, don't dress like a hooker. I'm into athletic, confident women, not insecure thots."

*Oh…you…*I growl inside my head. *I'm gonna remove your furry man-nuggets, fry them up, and feed 'em to feral pigs while you watch!*

He adds, "Plus, clearly you don't have the tits to pull off the whole cleavage-wallet thing, so…"

What does he know about cleavage wallets? I narrow my eyes at his handsome face, which includes a strong jaw and elegantly pronounced cheekbones—*so annoying!*—thinking about all the ways I'd like to painfully end him.

"Careful there, Mitch, or you just might find yourself alone with a psycho and no one there to stop him. Or her. Yeah, likely a her, since we all know you don't respect women. I bet your face is super popular on dartboards across the globe."

He chuckles like he's won some giant prize in the world's greatest asshole competition. "You've just proven my point. Sheilas don't mix with bodyguarding. Too emotional."

Grrrr… "Game on."

"Last time I checked, my life wasn't a game. Are you asking me to gamble with it so you can prove some fema-Nazi agenda?"

I. Want. To. Hurt. Him. "I'm egalitarian, not a fema-Nazi. And I'll remind you, Mr. Guppy Bubbles, that I'm putting my life on the line here, so—"

"Sir," Phil interrupts, "what time did you say you want to be at the fundraiser tonight?" Phil glances over his shoulder and gives me a "shut your piehole" look.

Dammit. I was crossing the line, and I know it, but *whatthehell!* Mitch is a cretin, and someone needs to put him in his place.

"Eight," Mitch replies.

"Thank you, sir," says Phil. "I need to make some personnel changes for the detail tonight and just wanted to ensure no one's late."

Fuck. That wasn't a hint coming from Phil just now. That was a flat out "you're fired."

I turn my head and look out the window. *Shit. Shit. Shit. I can't lose this job.* Sadly, I have no one to blame but myself. I let the Bulge get to me. I just don't get why I feel so amped up and emotional in his presence. I'm over him. I'm over us.

After passing the security gate at Mitch's house, the limo pulls up to the iron front door. It's a two-story, modernist home with tons of trees and tall hedges for privacy. The ten-foot iron fence enclosing the property has sensors and cameras for added security, but two guards patrol the property twenty-four seven to prevent anyone from getting through. The interior is equipped with a state-of-the-art alarm system that includes retractable steel shutters on all of the windows and doors in case of the need to do a lockdown. Whoever built the home was super paranoid or just loved *The Purge* look, though I will say I like the full gym, large chef's kitchen, and theater room. I got the tour during my last visit, including the upstairs, which I won't think about. *That whole night was a mistake, and now my anger over it just cost me my job.*

The driver comes around to let Mitch out.

"Nice knowing you, Grape Gum," he says as he slides out, prouder than a peacock.

I glare. "See ya, Guppy Bubbles."

He shakes his head, annoyed. "What's with the Guppy Bubbles?"

I narrow my eyes. "Because that's all you'll ever be to me. A tiny fish who farts his way through life."

He laughs. "Good one, Blabi." He slams the door shut, leaving me there with a snarl on my lips. Blabi is my nickname from high school. It was a joke since I never spoke to anyone aside from Georgie. I told him about it the night of the party.

Wait! What a faker! He remembers me.

CHAPTER FIVE

"Abi, you didn't even last one car ride?" Sam growls over the phone while I pace outside in a corner of Mitch's manicured yard complete with Olympic-sized pool, organic garden, greenhouse, outdoor kitchen, three gazebos, and a pool house. It's like a damned resort back here.

"I'm sorry, Sam, but you should've heard what he said. I mean, he practically called me stupid and said I was useless. All because I'm a woman."

Silence.

"Sam! You're supposed to say he's wrong. You're supposed to—"

"What, Abi? Tell Mitch to stop being a shallow, chauvinistic prick?"

"Well…yeah."

"This is the job," he says. "Sometimes the clients are pigs. Sometimes they'll be saints. It's not our place to go around playing God, judging people, and deciding whose lives are worth saving. We protect them, and as long as they don't cross any lines with my staff or break the law, they can think what they want."

"I seriously can't believe you right now," I grumble. "What would Georgie say if she knew I was being treated like a piece of shit?"

"She'd probably chew me the hell out, and then I'd remind her that there's a reason the job pays so damned much—it's commensurate for the work—and that the best way for you to prove Mitch wrong is to *prove* him the hell wrong. Do a good job. Be professional. Show him how strong you are, Abi."

Dammit! Sam has a point.

He adds, "As long as Mitch sticks to our protocols, then I have no reason to cancel the contract."

Ugh. The contract. It's more like an encyclopedia that outlines liabilities, waivers, the client's responsibilities to follow safety procedures, and such. It also spells out the rules of conduct between the client and staff. Basically, no touching unless it's to safeguard the client's body. Don't be a dumbass and run into an unsecure location and then expect the detail to protect the client, yadda yadda. Oh, and absolutely no fraternizing.

"The rules say the client can't verbally abuse the staff," I point out.

"He was being an ignorant jerk, not abusive, but if it makes you happy, I'll terminate with Mitch."

"Really?"

"No! If I do that, you don't get paid. I don't get paid. My company folds before it's even started, and Mitch will be dead by the end of the week. All because you couldn't handle a little macho stupidity."

Suddenly, it all hits home. This isn't a regular job. We aren't playing dress up and running simulations like in Alaska. This is life or death.

"Abi, I don't have anyone else who can blend in seamlessly with Mitch's social circle, so you need to ask yourself which is more important, your ego or his life? Because while I understand your feelings, the guy I know also has a good heart and doesn't deserve to be sentenced to death."

I pause and whoosh out a breath. "Can you at least talk to him? I mean, it's in his best interest not to piss me off when I should be keeping an eye on everyone around us."

"I'll talk to him, but don't get your hopes up. For whatever reason, he has a thing against women guarding him. You specifically. So just stick to your training and everything will be fine."

True. I had to sit five, six hours at a time under a frozen bush or up in a tree. The trainers said that while I would likely never be posted on a branch like a real owl, behaving like one would teach me two things: One, to endure extreme discomfort, and two, how to stay present and alert while literally dying of boredom. The thing about being a bodyguard is that you spend a lot of time doing absolutely nothing. You stand outside a door. You sit in a car. Even when you know you're in the safest place possible, it's your job to resist whipping out your phone to catch up on that latest romance novel you've been dying to read. *Sigh...* Fanged Love, Part Three. *When will I get to read it?*

"Okay. I'll behave," I say.

"Promise?"

"This is the last time we'll have this conversation. I swear."

"All right," Sam says skeptically. "But no more slipups. The situation is far too dangerous."

"Got it."

"And try to keep conversations with Mitch to a minimum. You're an owl, so there's no real reason to talk to him anyway. Just hang back behind the other girls. Look like you're too in awe of him to speak."

Eesh... "Will do. And, Sam? Thank you for giving me this chance."

"You can thank me by being careful. Keep those eyes and ears open."

"Hoo hoo," I sing like an owl.

"Good bird. Oh damn. I gotta go. Someone's calling on the other line." He ends the conversation, and I stand there in Mitch's backyard, growling at the wind.

I got this. I got this. I store my phone in my magic cleavage and head into the house. Obviously, I've been here once before—the night of the party—so I kind of know my way around, but after I enter the huge kitchen with two large fridges, two dishwashers, and two sets of ovens for entertaining, I make a wrong turn. I stop and look over my shoulder. This is the hallway that leads to the garage. I think?

I'm about to turn back when I hear Mitch's deep voice rumbling on the other side of a door that I assumed was just a closet. Must be a den or home office.

"Sam, I'm not spending the rest of my life running from that wanker. If he wants me, he can come get me." There's a long stretch of silence and then, "All I'm asking is that you find a bloke. I don't want that damned sheila guarding me."

Oh...you... I want to sock him.

Mitch adds, "Yeah, mate, I get why you picked her, but she's more likely to bloody leave me cactus than protect me. I was a complete *asshole* to her."

Cactus? I really need to get up to speed on Australian slang.

Long pause.

"Yeah, yeah," Mitch says. "I'll let you do your job, eh. But if I end up looking like a Swiss cheese, it'll be your nuts. Cheers," Mitch says, and the door swings open. His shock from finding me standing there is quickly eclipsed by outrage. "You were listening to my conversation?"

"No." I shake my head, likely looking guilty as sin. "I was just passing by and got turned around."

He narrows those vibrant eyes, which seem more like a mosaic of honey browns and sage greens than a solid color I could call hazel. "I have that piss-up at eight. Stay away and we won't have any trouble. Right?"

"Piss-up?" I ask.

"Party."

"Oh. Got it." I bob my head.

He struts off and leaves me standing there, wondering why my existence offends him. I wasn't the one who acted like a coldhearted ass. I didn't pretend I was genuinely interested and then say I never wanted to see him. So why is he being so hostile?

I make two fists and take a soothing breath. *I got this.*

CHAPTER SIX

Around six o'clock, after giving Phil my location assessment—which he said was flawless because it included all of the windows on both floors as points of possible entry (pats self on back)—I leave Mitch's house and head home. I need food, a nap, and a long hot shower before I'm sent back out into Mitch-world for another round of Abi bashing. Thankfully, I barely saw him all day, though I did spend a few hours in his private living room, just off his bedroom, while he did whatever. Like Phil said, spending time near him would create the illusion of being his sex-pet.

Blech!

I used the time to do research on my business plan. I suppose that's going to be the silver lining out of all this; over the next year working as a bodyguard, I am going to make enough money to cover almost everything—my mom's debt and my final semester of tuition. Maybe I'll even have a little left over to start up my nonprofit to help widows with financial problems, though most of that money will have to be funded through donations and small grants. I hope? It's going to take a lot of cash to help people refinance their lives. Still, knowing exactly what my goals are will help me get through this.

And prevent me from throttling the Bulge. Seriously, what a ridiculous nickname. So what if the man is hung? Don't see ladies with big clits going around calling themselves Clitzilla. How about big-breasted women? Even famous actresses or musicians, like Dolly Parton, known for ample bosoms don't refer to themselves by their body parts even if they're proud of what the good Lord gave them. But Mr. Shlongaconda? Total attention whore.

I want so badly to tell Georgie, my best friend and Sam's fiancée, how peeved I am that Mitch is my first assignment, but I can't talk about our clients. Not even to her. Still, I need a friend to lean on, and she's my nerd-sister from another nerd-mister.

With one fluffy towel wrapped around my wet hair and the other around my freshly moisturized body, I grab my cell from my white comforter, where I tossed it along with everything when I came home. I need to hear Georgie's voice.

"OMG! Abi! How'd it go with Mitch?" Georgie screams through the phone.

"Wait. You know?"

"Sam told me at Christmas. I've been dying to talk to you about it, but he made me promise to wait until he had a chance to spill the beans."

"I can't believe you knew…" I say under my breath and start digging through my closet—the section with my new tacky work clothes. "You're my best friend, and it didn't occur to you to break your promise to your fiancé?"

"Ohellno."

"Traitor," I grumble and pluck out the purple dress. It's super short with a deep V in the front. Guess I'm going braless tonight.

"But if I'd broken my promise to Sam, then you'd be wondering what sort of promises I'd break to you. Can't have that. Especially now that you're working for my fiancé. You both have to know you can trust me."

True, but… "How the hell do you do that?"

"What?" she asks.

"Make your betrayal sound like loyalty to me?"

Georgie chuckles. "It's a gift. But don't let that detract from the truth. I'm a trustworthy person."

"Says the woman who used a fake name to get an internship and hide it from her siblings."

"Whoa. Whoa… Those were extenuating circumstances."

She's actually right, and I don't know one single person who'd argue. Last year, her father kidnapped her entire family just to make himself look bonkers and avoid prosecution for creating an artificial shortage of life-saving cancer drugs. With prices shooting through the roof, he sold the pills on the black market for full price, versus the discounted rate paid by insurance companies.

Bastard.

Thing is, before he got caught, Chester Walton was a mega-billionaire and Texas oil mogul. His wife came from one of the wealthiest families in the state. He didn't need more money, but he cheated sick people just to get more of it. Now he's in prison, the holdings company broken up and sold off. Georgie, her big brother Henry, the two other sisters, and their mom kept the parts of the company they believed in—cancer-treatment pharmaceuticals, biofuel, and a few others. But before the breakup, Georgie had been looking for a way to help her siblings keep the holdings company intact while they brought their father to justice. She thought that meant proving her leadership skills to her siblings so she could help run some of the business. That was how she ended up interning for Sam McDaniel under a fake identity. It was a risky idea but became the turning point in her powerless life. She found her voice. Then she found the love of her life. Now she's working with her sister-in-law, Elle, to farm algae as a sustainable fuel source.

"Okay, G-cow," I say. "I'll forgive you for not telling me that Mitch was going to be my first client, so you can still be my friend. But don't mistake my tolerance of your whorey ways as acceptance." G-cow is one of my many, many nicknames for her. This one in particular started in high school when she went through her "I'm too fat" stage. She's never been fat. I thought it was funny until I went through my own and she started calling me Flabi. Blabi is another version—a joke from before I learned to talk to other human beings besides Georgie.

Georgie laughs. "Suck it, crunt. You know you love me."

"Crunt?"

"It means crusty cunt. It's new. Just made it up."

"Ooh. Good one." Yes, we can get super raunchy sometimes, but what do you expect from two nerds who grew up barely saying a word to anyone but each other? Behind closed doors, we said it all. We fantasized about the lives we'd live. We cussed like two pirates at a rum festival.

"Thanks. Now tell me what happened!" She squeals.

"Stop. You're giddying. No giddying."

"But…Mitch." She sighs with contentment. "So. Hot."

"Uh, so ewww. He's a pig."

"I'm not defending his bewildering ways, but I saw the two of you at the party."

"So?" I seriously don't know what she's getting at.

"So…there were sparks lighting up that corner of the room where you two were making out."

"Those weren't sparks. They were warning flares from the universe. I just couldn't see them because I was blinded by Mitch's male-superiority complex. Did you know it glows neon green in the dark?"

"What glows?"

"His complex. It's so toxic that it's like some radioactive leprosy that eats away at the female brain. It's how he gets so many women to sleep with him."

She laughs. "Oh, so now he's a disease?"

"I'm lucky to be alive," I say as a matter of fact.

"While I couldn't be more grateful that my best friend wasn't turned into a phosphorescent sex doll by this well-endowed monster of epic hotness, I think she might be overvilifying the man. Just a tad."

"Bite your tongue." I hang my damp towel on the little hook next to the door. I like my things neat and organized, which is why when my mom redid my room a few years ago, she added an entire wall of white storage cubes with linen baskets.

"I'm being serious, Abi. Sam is an excellent judge of character, and I doubt he'd be friends with Mitch if he were that rotten of a human being."

But Sam didn't defend Mitch when I brought the issue up. In fact, he confirmed that Mitch has a thing against female bodyguards. In other words, Sam knows Mitch isn't an angel.

"All I'm saying," she adds, "is that I think there's more to the story."

I slide on a black lace thong. "He's a turdler, so if you believe otherwise, then there's something you're not telling me."

"No. There isn't. Let's just drop it."

"Don't do that," I scold. "Why do you think I'm the one who's in the wrong here?"

"I didn't say you're in the wrong. I just said that I don't think Mitch is as bad as you think. I mean, remember how nice he was to us at his party? He even groveled about the slipup when I didn't get in."

My name had been on the guest list since Mitch's cousin, who I had an accounting class with, invited me. But my plus one had been left off the list. The security guard wouldn't let Georgie in, so I went looking for Mitch's cousin to see what could be done. I found the cousin and Mitch together. That was the first time we met, and it was one of those nonverbal "Well, who are you and where have you been all of my life?" moments. For both of us, I thought. Because neither he nor I could stop smiling or looking at each other. Mitch made sure Georgie got in and then didn't leave my side the entire night.

"Yeah, well…maybe he was nice because you're Georgie Walton," I offer.

"*Pfft!* My name might impress some people, but Mitch hangs out with rich, hot heiresses all the time."

I want to roll my eyes. "Fine. He's a real giver. A saint. When do you want to submit his application to the church?"

"Oh stop. There has to be a reason for what happened between you. Why not just ask him?"

"Right. I'm just going to walk up and say, 'Hey, Mitch. Remember how you pulled me out of bed, threw my panties at me, and shoved me out your front door before slamming it in my face?'"

Georgie gasps. "No! Say he didn't."

"Did," I throw back.

"How come you never told me that part?" she asks.

"Why the hell do you think? It's super embarrassing!" I step into the purple dress and zip up the side. I do a swivel in front of my full-length mirror in the corner. *Man, this is short.*

Georgie groans on the other end of the phone. "I'm so sorry, Abi. I honestly didn't know. I mean…I thought he just did the whole 'call you tomorrow' thing and then conveniently lost your number."

"Nope."

"I don't get it. He doesn't seem that cold."

"Well, he is." And no amount of Georgie optimism is going to change my mind about him.

"I need to tell Sam."

"While I'm thrilled that I've won this little debate and brought you into my camp of the Mitch haters, why would you tell Sam?" I remove the towel from my head and get to work with a comb on my wet hair. I'm going to have to blow-dry it and pull it up; otherwise it's going to take another hour to get ready, and I want to hang out with my mom a little before I take off.

"Sam thinks you two just didn't hit it off in the relationship department."

"Why would he think that?" I ask.

"I dunno. Mitch apparently said something about you being too good for him."

Huh? "Well, that's partially true. I *am* too good for him, but that's not why he chucked me like a putrid egg." Not that I have a clue about the real reason. Nor do I give two turds.

"Oh, Abi." Georgie sighs. "I'm so sorry."

"Don't be. You didn't know." Honestly, I just wanted to move on as quickly as possible. I mean, yeah, the encounter was magical. I felt like I'd found my soul mate that night.

Damn, someone should write a bad country song about it...Kissed at dusk. Dumped at dawn. Pumped my heart into a sad, sad song. And cue twangy slide guitar.

"Georgie," I say, "I know you won't agree with this, but you can't tell Sam. Not ever."

"Abi! Why? He needs to know what kind of guy Mitch is."

My mind points to an earlier convo with Sam. More or less, he said that unless the client is crossing some serious lines, then he's not going to be cancelling any contracts. And, the truth is, I need this job. Not want. Need. Besides, what happened between me and Mitch is personal. Guarding him is business. The two are and should remain separate.

"Sorry, Georgie," I say, "but I am prohibiting you from saying anything to my boss."

She groans. "Fine. I won't tell Sam. But you really should mention something yourself."

I kinda already did, and Sam wouldn't listen. Of course, Georgie could get through to him, but I'm not going to put a wedge between my best friend and the love of her life. Sam is a good guy, so despite how I feel about dickosaurus, I have zero desire to fuck up Sam's new business.

"Thanks, girl," I say. "And if it makes you feel any better, I'm okay with all this. Other than Mitch being a sleaze, I like the job."

"Really?"

"Yeah." I slide my feet into a pair of black heels. "I get to carry a gun, dress like a stripper, and say stupid things. It's like facing every fear I've ever had and then being forced to make peace with them."

"Oh-kayyy."

"No. Really. I've always been afraid of saying something lame and everyone judging me. Now I get paid to do it. Sorta takes the sting out of making an unintentional jackass out of myself. Do it enough times on purpose, you're immune. Plus, I've always wondered what it would feel like to have men just look at me like a piece of eye candy."

"And?"

"I'll find out tonight," I reply. "My dress is so tight you can see my ovaries. It's very seductive," I joke.

"Where are you putting your gun?"

"I'm using that little sparkly black purse you got me for Christmas. It's the perfect size."

I still can't believe I even have one. A gun, that is. But oddly, I like knowing I can protect anyone, anywhere, at any time despite my five-five height and smaller female frame. I'm a good guy, and the world needs more of us, ready to stop the would-be attacker, the thug, the rapist. But, truthfully, I wouldn't feel this way had I not spent one month with four skilled riflemen and target shooters. Jack, our head instructor, was rated the best long-distance shot six years in a row at some international competition. Rumor has it from the other instructors that he spent fifteen years in the CIA as a weapons trainer. The point is that I'm well trained for an average, everyday Jane, and I would never treat a gun like a toy. Can't say the same for everyone out there.

"Well, just be careful," she says. "I don't know what I'd do if anything happened to you."

"I'll be fine. The job is actually kind of exciting. Way better than my summer job at Taco World, working for that jerk Lester." Worst boss ever. He yelled at me every five seconds. It got so bad I finally told him to fuck himself and quit. Ironically, though, working for him became this big turning point in my life. I started standing up for myself and getting heavily involved at school. I felt like if I could stand up to Lester and face him, I could face anyone. I still hate public speaking though. Standing in front of a crowd terrifies me. It's the one thing I won't do. Not ever.

She chuckles. "I think you're perfect for your new job, Abi."

"Someone has to protect these weak men, right?"

"Ha! Right?" She laughs. "Poor Mitch. I dare him to kick you out on your ass again."

I smile. "I don't think he'd dare. But thankfully, I'm just helping with surveillance. Technically, I don't even have to talk to him."

"Good luck with that. It's clear you still have a lot to get off your chest, not that I blame you. Just wait for the right time; otherwise—"

"I'm not getting canned. Not for him." I start loading up my purse with the essentials. Lipstick, driver's license—yes, I have one, but I don't own a car since I had to sell it for cash—Band Aids for my foot in case I get blisters from my heels, and some Tylenol for the headache I'm going to get from being in the same room with Mitch all night.

"Good. Glad to hear it. By the way, has Sam told you about the trip to Miami?"

"Miami?" I freeze, almost dropping the phone. "You mean the one in Florida?"

"No, the Miami down the street. Yes, Florida! It's for some big photo-shoot fashion-show thing."

I groan. I really don't want to take any road

trips with Mitch. The hours will be long and there'll be no escape. At least here in Houston I can come home at the end of my shift and decompress. Plus, I'll miss my nightly dinner chats with my mom.

"Oops," Georgie says. "Guess Sam forgot to mention it. Mitch has to make an appearance for some swimsuit thing, which you'll get to go to."

I sigh with defeat. "Sounds spectacular."

"Yes, but..."

"What?" I feel the dread creeping in.

"Sam feels like the risk is really high. He tried to talk Mitch out of going, but that man is stubborn. He refuses to change a minute of his life because of these threats. And, don't hate me, but I overheard Sam telling Phil that he's considering having you glued to Mitch's side."

"What? I'm supposed to be the owl. Eyes and ears only!" I feel my arms and legs tingle as anger pumps through me.

"Guess you're getting a promotion?" she says awkwardly.

Great. Just...great. I'm going to kill Sam. This was not the deal.

"I have to go, Georgie. The Bulge is going to some fundraiser party tonight, and I need to finish putting together my '80s ho disguise." Plus, my mom made lasagna to welcome me home. I just don't know what I'm going to tell her when she starts asking questions about my new job or the monthlong training in Alaska. I hate lying to her.

"Oh no. You're going to the charity party at The Sterling?" Georgie asks.

"Yes. Wait. How do you know?"

"Gotta go! Love you. Mean it. Bye." The call ends, and I stare at the phone in disbelief. I feel like life can be cyclical sometimes—i.e., good things come in waves, just like bad things—but lately I feel the universe is having a little fun at my expense. "*Today is poke-Abi-in-the-butthole day. Tomorrow will be kick-her-in-the-shin day, followed by a biiig hug! She'll never know what hit her!*"

I text Sam and ask what he's not telling me about this party, but by the time I'm dressed and finished eating over an awkward game of "dodge the question" with my mom, it's an hour later and he still hasn't responded.

Well, it's only a party. How bad can it be? Then again, Sam has been making a habit out of not telling me things until the very last moment.

CHAPTER SEVEN

"Can you repeat that?" I say to the tuxedo-wearing greeter at the door of The Sterling, a luxury golf resort forty minutes north of Houston in The Woodlands. It's the type of place where companies hold big conferences and political groups raise money by offering-pro-golf weekends.

"Miss, it's a charity event for dolphins." The man points to a big sign propped up beside the door. There's a Photoshopped picture of Mitch in his swimsuit, strategically cropped at the waist for decency purposes, I assume. His arm is wrapped around a giant dolphin, like they're BFFs, and it reads *Dolphins are our mates, mate! So bring yours and enjoy an evening of music, pints, and an auction to raise money for the Hofer Dolphin Sanctuary.*

I crinkle my nose. *Oh…so now he's a dolphin lover, huh? Right. Sure he is.* Mitch Hofer cares only about himself.

"Okay," I say, "I see the sign. Think I'm up to speed on that. Now can you go over that other part? The one about me having to be tied to another human being all night?"

"The event planners are trying to capitalize on Mr. Hofer's nationality. They wanted to give the party an Australian flair, *mate*." He holds out two blue and red ribbons. "And you'll need to be tied to yours in order to get in."

"What? I am not going to be lassoed to someone all night. What if I have to go to the bathroom?"

"Look, lady, I'm just working the event. I don't come up with the themes. If you want in, you have to be tied to a partner."

"Well…I'm supposed to meet someone here. Inside." Sam actually told me to wait for him outside. He just failed to mention why.

He dips his head, giving me a look like he's not buying it. "If you've come alone, please step to the side, and you will be paired with the first single person."

"What is this, a roller coaster?" I suddenly notice the long line of partygoers, all bound at the wrists in Aussie-flag-colored ribbons.

"Fine." I hold up my hands. "I'll wait over here." I step aside, grab my cell, and shoot off a text to Sam, asking where he is because I can't get into the party, which means I can't hoot, hoot, hoot for him.

Sam: *Sorry. Had emergency w/ other client. Sending team member now to meet you. I'll be along shortly to check in on things.*

Phil is in charge of the team, so I wonder why Sam is coming at all, other than he wants to see me in action.

> ***Me:*** *How will you get in? Must have mate to enter.*
>
> ***Sam:*** *Have special pass.*
>
> ***Me:*** *Okay. See you here.*

Just as the dots are flickering on my screen, I hear a deep voice from behind me. "Are you Abi?"

I turn and see an incredibly gorgeous man approach. He looks like he just flew in from the set of a Bond movie—his hair perfectly cut and styled, his skin with just the right amount of golden glow, and the most charming smile I've ever seen.

Wow. Just... I shake my head. *Wow!*

"Looks like I'm late. The party's already started," he says. "I always seem to get caught up in your wretched traffic."

Oh...he's British. He's also tall, swarthy, and debonair. I'm smitten.

"Sorry, but you are...?" I ask quietly as the line of well-dressed partygoers stream by and enter the ballroom.

"Leland Merrick, at your service." He extends his hand, and when I offer mine, he presses his soft lips to the top of my hand. I literally shiver. It feels like he just smooched the back of my knees.

Oh, God. I'm too hot-man-whipped to think straight. "Bahgood. Meetyou. Me. Hello?"

He winks those twinkling chocolate brown eyes with golden flecks. A shameless, unapologetic pair of dimples pucker in his cheeks. "Lovely to meet you as well, Abi," he says, all politeness with a crisp accent.

I lean in close. "So what's your position?"

I'm thinking he might be a wolf? Those are the team members who actively hunt threats, versus my passive role. The peacocks are people like Phil, out front, showing their feathers.

He leans in to whisper in my ear, gently sliding his smooth cheek against mine, which ignites another delicious shiver. "I can do whatever position you like, Abi. No one mentioned how beautiful you are."

My heart starts to pound like a horny fist wanting to break through the wall that's preventing me from getting a raging case of goo-goo eyes.

I nod dumbly. "Uh. Yeah. You too?"

He stands tall, breathing into his wide chest like a rooster out to conquer. "Such a nice compliment from a nice girl." He holds out his elbow. "Shall we mate, love?"

Yesss, please. I'll even let you be on top. I bob my head.

"Lovely." He steps forward and says a bunch of things to the guy at the door. I'm seriously not paying attention. Leland is…well, he looks like if Momoa, Mr. Darcy, and 007 all pitched in to create a super baby and that baby was raised by alpha males and princes, until one day he became the man standing before me. Flagrantly masculine and sexual, wrapped in a fine suit.

Before I know it, my wrist is tethered to the only man in the room capable of pulling my attention away from the host, who's standing just a few feet away, posing for selfies with the guests alongside someone in a cheesy dolphin costume.

I know I'm here at this party for a reason, but the moment is too magical to do my job. Being on the arm of this god makes me wonder if this is what it feels like to be plucked out of the crowd by your favorite actor as he walks down the red carpet on Oscar night. Suddenly, you catch his eye. He walks toward you and reaches through the mass of photographers, summoning you, wondering where you've been his entire life. "*From this day forward, we shall never part.*"

I sigh. It's the lamest romantic fantasy ever, but it's mine. So is the one where Captain Kirk is Idris Elba, and I'm the green Orion lady.

"Ah, here is our table," Leland says, pulling out my chair with his free arm. "Can I bring you a cocktail, love?"

"Love…" I swoon, taking my seat. "I'll have champagne."

"Champagne it is." He unties our wrists. "Back in a flash."

"Okay," I mutter and watch him saunter off to the far corner of the room.

"Abi, who is that?" Mitch is suddenly hovering

over me, an ugly snarl on his sex-lips. "And what the hell are you wearing?"

"Huh?" Still seated, I blink up at him.

"You're supposed to be here as part of my entourage." He looks over his shoulder at the group of tall blondes giggling and having the time of their lives. They're all tied together in one long chain. He leans in. "And I thought I made myself clear; I don't date women who dress like they're out to make a buck."

My face flushes with angry heat. So many words come to mind in this moment, but none quite capture my feelings because such a word doesn't exist. *Motherfuckerbuttholebastardpigfacecaveman.* But I'm an educated woman. My mother taught me to take the high road like a lady. *Or, in this case, annoy the hell out of him just for fun.*

"Sorry. Do I know you?" I say, patting the side of my hair, which is pinned up in a twist.

Mitch narrows those hazel eyes with thick caramel brown lashes. "Don't make me call Sam."

And cut my evening short with the Greek god from steamingpantyopolous? I think not!

"Shoo, wet wipe," I hiss. "Sam asked me to crowd-blend tonight. You're blowing my cover. And just plain blowing." I mumble that last part.

This time, he leans all the way down, getting in close. His supple lips graze my ear, and it sends a sinful shock wave through my body. I don't want him. I don't. But goddammit, the smell of his skin and the feel of his lips on my earlobe instantly propel me back to our night together—his naked body on top of me, his hands touching my tight nipples, his heated breath bathing my neck.

"I can get you fired in two seconds, Abi. Don't push me," he says.

The memory shatters like a wineglass dropped to the floor. *And...I'm back.*

"Wow." I lean away, but keep my voice low. "So you almost fuck me and then you chuck me. And now you want me and my mother to lose our house because I'm pretending to be with a date at a party where I'm working to protect you? If only I were a dolphin, maybe you'd be just a little more human."

"Final warning, Abi," he growls. "I don't need this drama or your guilt trips."

"Uh, hello. I speak the truth. Sorry if it offends you because you're so used to having your ass kissed."

His hateful expression softens. "Are you really about to be homeless?"

"What do you care, Mitch?"

"Don't say that," he mutters softly, a hint of shame in his tone.

"Say what?" I stand and face him.

"Abi love, is everything all right?" Leland appears at my side. It's a guy thing, but his stance—slightly overlapping my body and wedging himself a few inches between me and Mitch—signals that I belong to him and Mitch should shake a tail.

"Yeah." I nod. "I'm fine. The host of this really cool event was introducing himself. But I just told Mr. Hofer here that I already donated everything I can. I'm tapped out."

Leland takes my hand. "Then I'm certain our humble host won't mind if I steal you away to the dance floor so he can solicit money elsewhere."

I lean toward Mitch and whisper, "Off you go, pooker. Go do your thing and let us do ours." I saunter away with my hawt AF date. I'm going to have to thank Sam for this gift of a partner.

Leland and I take our place in the center of the dance floor, which is at the far end of the room next to the floor-to-ceiling French-style windows overlooking the terrace. Outside, several groups of guests are mingling and puffing on cigarettes under a large trellis covered with twinkling lights. I take note once again of how easy it would be to sneak in here from the hotel's gardens. Checking the grounds was the first thing I did when I arrived.

I slide my hand into Leland's and gaze into his warm, dark eyes. It's no exaggeration when I say that every female eye in the room is on either him or Mitch. For the record, the two are tied in the looks department. Solid tens. But I have to deduct five points for Mitch's personality and lack of character.

"So," I whisper, swaying in time to Leland's six-foot frame, "how long have you worked for Sam?"

Leland's smile looks forced all of a sudden, like

he doesn't know what to say, so he's opting to charm my brain into a muddled state. It might be working.

No, no, no. Stay focused, little bird. I'm here to work. I need to start taking a mental inventory of everyone in the room. I know Phil is lurking somewhere and will be expecting me to take a break in the ladies' room. I have to text him my location assessment. Specifically, I need to flag anyone suspicious.

Oh, like that woman. She's standing against the wall, staring hungrily at Mitch across the room. She looks like she wants to bang him and then maybe dice him up and bake him in a pie. She also appears to be completely alone.

I make a mental note: *Y, F, 40, purple dress, 5.*

Phil will know I'm raising a yellow flag (Y) for a suspicious-looking female (F) in her forties (40), last seen at the southeast corner of the room—the five-o'clock position (5).

Leland slowly turns to me, and I look at him expectantly. He still hasn't answered my question. Nor is he doing a visual sweep of the room.

Huh. That's strange. Maybe he's done his already? He did just turn me so he could see the rest of the room.

"So…how long?" I ask again.

"Sorry, dove?"

"Sam. You. How long have you been working for him?" I repeat.

Again, he holds that smile like a shield. "Well, you know…long enough. And yourself?"

He doesn't want to tell me. Maybe he's new and doesn't want to come off as weak or lesser in my eyes?

"I just started today, actually," I say.

"Oh. Really? So this must be very exciting for you, playing bodyguard to such a big celebrity. Any updates on the people who are after Mr. Hofer? I hear they'll stop at nothing, so I'm guessing it's going to be high alert for some time."

Wait a sec. Why would Leland say that? If he's on Sam's team, then he knows the specifics are classified.

Why? Sam won't say.

So if Leland knows that, then why ask me? Sam would tell us if he had any additional information to share.

My phone vibrates in my sparkly little purse. "One sec. I have to catch this." I dig the thing out and glance at the screen.

> **Sam:** *Ronald is outside waiting. Where R U? He can't get into the party.*

Ronald. Ronald is my date for tonight? I've never met the man, but if he's outside waiting for me, then who the hell is this guy?

I look at Leland and try not to show my panic. *Oh fuck. Oh fuck. This guy isn't part of our team!* This guy is here to kill Mitch?

A tiny part of my sad horny heart dies with a twitch. *Why! Why? He's so hot.* No joke. I freaking hate it in movies when the crazy-good-looking hero turns out to be the bad guy. Such a waste.

I quickly get into character like the trainer told me. "*Remember, Abi, when there's a threat, your job isn't to step in, play the hero, or get involved. Leave that to the lead bodyguards with years of experience. You become a fly on the wall. You stay in character: act dumb, oblivious, whatever feels appropriate for the setting that makes you invisible to any persons of interest.*"

How am I supposed to do that? Leland already knows I'm working for Sam. How? Great question. But I can't waste my time with it right now. I've got to tell Phil that I'm with R, M, 30, tux, 6. Red flag, male, in his thirties, wearing a tux, at six o'clock.

"Leland? Leland Merrick. That you?" A tall woman about my age, with long dark hair and wide green eyes, comes up to us. Her grin is downright hostile. "What are you doing here?"

Leland's plastic smile turns passive-aggressive, too. They both look like vicious pit bulls with a grinning problem.

"Gisselle, what a surprise," he says blandly. "Aren't you supposed to be halfway around the world by now?"

"Ha! You think I'd trust any information you feed me? Fat chance." She grabs his arm, but looks at me. "I'm so sorry. I need to speak with him for a moment."

"Errr...no problem. I need to hit the loo anyway."

She drags him off to the side of the room, eliciting a few judgmental stares from other guests. I watch them from behind a group of people near the restrooms. The two are whisper-fighting—finger shaking, red faces, and lots and lots of whispering.

Ohmygod. I bet they're rival hit men. They both want to kill Mitch. What else could it be? I head into the bathroom and call Phil. It's too urgent for a text.

"This'd better be good," Phil's deep voice snarls through the phone.

"M and F. Twenty, thirty, red. Red! Tux and little black dress. Sexy. At six. Or five. Wait. Make that three. They just moved."

"Abi, slow down. I can't understand you."

"Um. Okay." I start hyperventilating. "This really good-looking guy came up to me outside, and I thought he was sent by Sam to be my date, but he's not. My date is still outside waiting for me. But this guy, he knows I work for Sam. He was asking all kinds of questions about who's after the client. Then this woman came up to us, and I think she's here to kill Mitch, too."

"Can you describe them?" Phil asks.

"Well, he's hot. Really, really hot—"

"Abi! Physicals."

"Oh. Sorry. Um, six or six one. Dark hair.

Wearing a tux. He looks like he's about thirty. He's standing to the side of the dance floor, arguing with a pretty brunette in a black—"

"I see them. Go get Mitch. Quietly and calmly take him outside to the limo."

"Me?" My heart rate goes from panicked to imminent meltdown.

"Yes."

"But I'm just an ow—"

"Now!" he roars.

"Okay. Okay." The call ends, and I feel my head getting lighter. *Oh no.* I think I'm having a panic attack. I used to get them when I was in my early teens, just about the time I hit puberty. Boys started staring, and I would become overwhelmed with embarrassment, not knowing how to react or what to do. Being shy sucked hard. But it's been years since I've had a full-blown panic attack.

Suck it up, girl! You have to get Mitch. If I fail, he might die.

The door to the restroom swings open, almost crashing into me.

"Oh. Sorry, dear," says an older woman in a blue dress with black dolphins printed all over it. She takes one look at me, and her smile drops. "Dear, are you all right? I own cotton balls with more color."

I press my hands to my chest. "I. Can't. Breathe."

She grips me by the elbow to steady me. "I'll call

for an ambulance."

"No." I shake my head, gasping for air. "Just give me a second."

"Are you certain? I think I should—"

"No." I bend over. "But can you please…" Pant, pant, pant. "Go outside and tell Mr. Hofer he needs to get to the limo? Tell him…" Pant, pant, pant. "Abi said it's urgent, and I'll be there in a minute."

"If you insist, but are you sure you'll be all right, sweetie?" she asks.

"Yep. Hunky-dory. I just need a moment to catch my breath. I'll be right behind you."

"No need. I can entertain the Bulge just fine." She pushes me down into a chair next to the full-length mirror in the primping area. "You just rest and come along when you can."

"Thanks. You're a lifesaver." Of course, she's giddy as hell at the idea of spending time with Mitch.

She leaves the restroom, and I throw myself back in the chair, letting my arms flop to my sides and doing my best to make space in my tight lungs. *It's all in your head. It's all in your head. It's all in your…*

A splotch of mud on the beige tile floor catches my eye. It's fresh and in the exact spot where that woman was just standing.

Mud.

The garden.

Oh no!

I spring to my feet and dash out of the restroom into the crowded ballroom. Across the ocean of guests, I spot Mitch's tall frame as he bends his head to listen to the old woman.

Sneaky little nana!

"Excuse me! Excuse me!" I push my way through the mob of partygoers, leaving behind a trail of offended people. I literally feel like I'm about to black out from lack of oxygen, and I have to get to him quickly.

"Mitch!" I manage to scream. "She's…she's…" I grab the back of the woman's dress as I go down "…a killer."

CHAPTER EIGHT

MITCH

"Abi? Abi! Are you all right?" I pat her soft cheek, hoping to hell she's not going into some sort of damned cardiac arrest. "Abi, wake the bloody hell up."

"She's out cold," says Phil, the guy in charge of the team I'm paying to watch my ass. "Just make sure she keeps breathing until the ambulance gets here."

This guy is giving me orders? I'm the damned client. I'm paying for his bloody time. And how the fuck did he let this happen? That old goat almost put a bush knife in my chest.

I want to stand and pummel Phil, but that can wait. I need to make sure Abi is all right. Despite what she thinks, I do care about her.

"What the hell happened?" Sam charges through the crowd, looking more pissed off than I feel.

"Abi stopped that woman from carving me up like a ham," I growl and glance at the lady, who looks as sweet as any grandma. Igor, second in command, has her hands in zip ties.

"Let me go, you hooligan!" she yells. "Help! Somebody help! I'm being assaulted!"

Phil, Igor, and the event security warn everyone to stand back.

"I'm just an old woman. A fan. They're hurting me," she cries.

No one is buying it. Mostly because like me, everyone saw the crazy bat pull a fucking hunting blade from the front of her dress.

Now that's a cleavage purse. How the hell did she get it in there? It was half the length of her damned body. All I can say is that I'm relieved no one was hurt.

I glance down at Abi's face. She looks like a sexy angel—pink lips resting in a soft pucker, rosy cheeks, and an oval face that give her the appearance of innocence. It's what drew me to her the night we met—a face that tells you she's sweet and good and all the things a guy like me needs.

Right. That last part is bullshit. I might find Abi attractive, but I want nothing to do with her, which is the reason I kicked her out the morning after my party. *Thank bloody God I didn't fuck her.* That would make me the asshole she claims me to be. A man in my situation cannot afford to drag anyone into this mess, let alone a nice girl like Abi. I don't know what the hell I was thinking messing around with her in the first place, and I sure as fuck don't know what Sam was thinking hiring her.

Still crouching beside Abi, I snarl up at Sam, "Mate, I told you this would be a goddamned mistake. Now look at her!"

"Abi had the highest score of any person to ever pass that training," Sam argues. "And she saved your life." The look on his face says it all: *How about being grateful, you ass? You're alive. Thanks to her.*

"We're done here, mate. Bloody fucking done," I snarl at him. "I won't be having women getting mowed down to save me."

Sam bends down at my side and speaks quietly into my ear. "This was your idea, Mitch. Remember? Instead of witness protection, you wanted to carry on like nothing's happened. But it has. So let Phil and his team do their job. Let Abi do hers. And put your fucking ego aside."

Despite Sam being the only guy I trust, I am *this* close to putting my fist through his teeth. I chose not to be a giant pussy and hide for the rest of my life. It's why I pay him.

Except, it's not only your life at risk, is it? I glance down at Abi, whose warm brown eyes are beginning to flutter open. I should feel pleased that she's all right, but it only clears the path for my anger. If I had wanted her in harm's way, I would have fucked her and kept on doing it. Maybe I would have had a go at a real relationship. But I didn't.

I stand and face Sam. We're the same height, but he has more of a bulky build. I'm hard lean muscle. Except for a very small spot just below my navel—a leftover from my pudgy teen years. My trainer says no one sees it, but I do. It's a reminder that no matter how far I've come, I'm not perfect.

"We'll talk about this later." I leave before Abi witnesses me being pissed off. She can't know I give a damn. I want her as far away as possible. Her and everyone else who's not as deadly and ruthless as the people who want to kill me.

ABI

When I come to, Sam is standing over me, arguing with Mitch about something. It all sounds like garble. But the kicking and screaming coming from Granny Murder Pants is loud and clear.

I sit up and squeeze the sides of my head, willing the room to stop spinning.

"Take it easy, Abi. You fell pretty hard," says Sam, crouching beside me as Mitch marches away.

No "Thank you for saving my life"? No "Hey, I'm so glad you were here"? Why the hell does Mitch hate me so much that he can't even show a modicum of gratitude? *Oh. Wait. I know.* He's pissed because a woman just saved him. His giant ego can't handle it.

"You did good." Sam pushes some loose hair from my face, inspecting the mark.

"He doesn't seem to think so," I mutter, glancing at the exit.

Sam lets out a grumble. "Mitch is grateful. He's just not used to being saved by a woman."

"Jackass."

"Well, take it from another jackass, Mitch will come around. And when he does, he'll be thanking his lucky stars for you."

I opt to rub my pounding forehead rather than argue.

"By the way," Sam asks, "how did you know that woman was going to try to kill him?"

"Mud. She had mud on her shoes from the garden."

He stares for a moment and then gets it. "Well done."

"What about that man Leland? Did you catch him, too?" I ask.

"I'm sorry to say he won't be hauled off to jail tonight. He's actually a reporter and the biggest pain in my ass ever to walk the planet."

"A reporter?"

Sam nods. "And he has a way of digging up little facts, piecing together a hunch, and then tricking people into confirming or denying his assumptions."

Oh… So when he asked me those questions, he had been fishing. "And that woman, the brunette?"

"Gisselle, a rival of his. They both caught a whiff of Mitch's story and have been sniffing around ever since." Sam shakes his head. "Of course, they couldn't care less about how dangerous the situation is or that digging around might get someone killed.

They care more about scooping each other than a person's life."

I'm so stupid. I should have known. "I thought he was my date, sent by you."

"Did he give you the grape-gum code?"

Oh crap. I forgot. "No. I'm so sorry."

"Did you say anything?" Sam asks.

"I don't know..." I wince from the spanking I'm getting inside my head.

"Sorry. Sorry. Let's just get you to the doctor and then we can talk about all that."

"I'm fine," I say, extending my hand. "Just help me up."

"Abi..." Sam protests.

"Really. There's nothing wrong. Just got a little excited is all. I hyperventilated."

I can tell by Sam's flat lips that he doesn't believe me. Luckily, the police arrive to take Grandma Guillotine to jail, which stops the conversation right there.

"I'll call you later," Sam says to me and then looks at Phil. "Can you take Abi home?"

"What about the new night-watch team I'm supposed to train?" Phil asks.

Sam rubs his forehead like he's had a rough night. I know he's managing multiple events and teams. His plate is full, and Mitch's protection is probably sucking up more of his time than he'd planned.

I raise my hand. "I'll Uber. Don't worry."

"No. You just blacked out and—"

I start heading toward the exit. "All better. See? Catch you later, Sam!" I wave but don't look back.

I head toward the hotel lobby, grabbing my jacket from the coat check before going to the main driveway, where I spot Mitch getting in his limo. Two large men, who look extremely nervous with their swiveling heads, are keeping watch.

I turn away, hoping Mitch doesn't spot me. The last thing I want is more of this guy tonight.

"Abi!" Mitch calls out.

Great. I paste on a fake smile and wave to be polite before quickly going back to my phone to search for the Uber app.

"Woman, get in the car," he says.

Woman. Woman? Woman! My name is Abigail Carter, and I just saved your ass, big man. So how about a little respect?

"Uh, thanks, but I'm good." Wanting to keep my promise to Sam—no more drama—I point at my phone so Mitch gets the gist.

Suddenly, he's sliding out of his limo, walking toward me. "Abi, I can't leave you standing out here. It's not safe. And if tonight wasn't proof enough of how unsafe, I'll remind you that the woman who just tried to stab me was one of many after the bounty on my head."

Bounty? "Why? What did you do?"

He glares for a moment. "Who says I did anything?"

"Well," I shrug, "you are Mitch Hofer."

He doesn't speak. Not with his mouth anyway. His eyes say that I should tread carefully. My brain says that's a fresh invitation to fuck with him and...screw me! I can't resist.

"So what'd you do, huh?" I ask. "Did you paddle in some other man's pool? Turn down a banana-hammock contest sponsored by the mob? Wait, I know. You—"

"Get in the limo," he rumbles.

He doesn't get to tell me what to do. "No, thanks." I begin walking away. "I can take care of myself. And apparently, I can also take care of you. See you soon!"

"Not if I can help it!" he yells back.

Fine. Get me fired. What do I care? It's only ten thousand dollars a month, my house, my college education, and my dream. *Fuck. What am I doing?* Once again, I've let Mitch get under my skin and allowed my pride to speak for me when I should be keeping my eye on what's really important.

"Wait! I'm sorry," I yell, watching the limo pull away.

Dammit, Abi. Why did you have to go from wallflower to ballbuster? I've spent my entire life biting my tongue, and now it's like I've forgotten how.

With cell in hand, I shoot off a text to Georgie, asking if we can hang out. I need to decompress. I need to talk through this crazy-ass night.

Georgie: *I'm at the Hoof N' Brew with Elle and her friend Tass.*

I've never met Tass, but I've heard a lot about her, and a little bit of girl time is just what this bodyguard needs to clear her head. The truth is, Mitch's opinion or actions shouldn't matter so much, but clearly they do. I need to figure out why.

CHAPTER NINE

The Hoof N' Brew is the kind of bar most decent people steer clear of. It's dirty, loud, and the hardworking patrons take their unwinding seriously. Which is exactly why it's the kind of place a girl like Georgie can go and let loose. She belongs to one of the wealthiest families in the state, but is one of the most humble, genuine people I've ever met. Still, the press hounds her and the rest of her family day and night. I don't know how Sam or any of them puts up with it. As for this hole-in-the-wall, nobody from Georgie's high-society social circles would be caught dead here. Another small fact: her brother, Henry, owns the place.

Henry, who is a defensive end for the Texans, bought it after his new wife, Elle, complained that there was nowhere they could go to do normal things—like watch some football at a bar with friends. So, as a gift to her, he bought this shit-kicker bar about twenty minutes from their penthouse in downtown Houston, intending to close it to the public on days when they want to hang with friends and feel like they're out for some casual fun. But, after a few visits, Henry discovered that the rough-looking cowboy-biker bar was really more of a local watering hole, frequented by the sort of people who just like to kick back. Oh, and they hate outsiders. With a passion. So problem solved. The moment Henry bought the place and gave out a few rounds on the house, he and Elle were no longer outsiders. Now, when he's not playing, they get to enjoy Sunday suds while feeling like regular people instead of tabloid chow. The bar patrons get to enjoy beer, often free on the days Henry shows up, with one of their favorite football players while they make sure the riffraff stays out. Riffraff being sports reporters, stalkers, and paparazzi.

I pull into the parking lot filled with dusty pickup trucks and Harleys. A few semis are parked toward the far end of the lot, just below the billboard with the Hoof N' Brew logo—a bull giving a karate kick to a giant mug of frothy beer. The building itself is all dark wooden siding made to look like a barn, and a cheesy neon light flashes over the doorway. *21 and over.*

I pull open the solid door, and it creaks like a warm greeting from the bar itself. *Come…in…*

I step inside, and the entire room freezes. The only sounds come from the three widescreen TVs in separate corners of the establishment—one near the big bar, one near the pool tables, and the other toward the packed seating area filled with small round tables and wooden chairs. There's a mechanical bull in the center of the room that doesn't work. The lighting is dark, the floor is covered in hay, and the room smells like popcorn.

Oh, goodie. It's cheese-corn night.

"Abi!" Georgie raises her hand to flag my attention and likely signal to the other tribe members that I'm a welcome guest.

I jerk my head, slip off my gloves, and head to her table. I immediately spot Elle, who also happens to be Georgie's new supergenius sister-in-law. The brunette with a tiny frame, wearing thick glasses, has to be Tassie, Elle's once college roommate.

"So happy you came." Georgie stands and gives me a giant hug.

"Good evening, ladies," I chirp happily. "Thanks for letting me crash your night out. You have no idea how much I need this."

"You and me both, sister," Elle says. "This is my first time away from the baby."

I completely forgot. Elle gave birth to her and Henry's first child, a little girl, on Christmas Day. I also heard that Elle's mother, who'd been diagnosed with cancer, was officially declared to be in remission that same week. Georgie was really relieved because she adores Elle and she'd been through a lot with her mom's illness. It was time for everyone to catch a break.

"Congrats on the baby. What did you name her?" I ask Elle.

"Marie, after Marie Curie, the first woman to win a Nobel Prize for her work in physics." Elle offers a proud smile.

Very fitting name for a girl who's destined to be a superhuman given the combination of her parents' physical and mental attributes.

"Marie is an adorable name." I slide off my coat, and the three ladies' eyes almost pop out.

I look down at my skimpy purple dress. "Sorry. I just came from work." I plop down in the fourth wooden chair.

The three keep staring. My answer didn't explain enough apparently.

"Oh. Sorry. I'm a bodyguard, and tonight I had to go to some party, only my," I look at Georgie, "very *nice* boss didn't tell me it was an upscale fundraiser versus a party with more of a trashy theme."

"Oh no." Georgie winces, looking embarrassed on behalf of Sam. "Well, I know your boss—the sweet, kind, sexy man that he is—has been overwhelmed with his new company while raising his daughter, Joy."

Ugh. I often forget that Sam is a widower and single dad. The good thing is that he found Georgie, and she loves him as much as she loves Joy, who's four now. Their wedding is planned for June on the family yacht so the press can't sneak into the event. They're keeping the location a secret until the last minute—I'm talking…morning of the wedding.

We're all supposed to meet at some private airport, ready to go. I love how the event feels like a tribute to their relationship. They're determined to do things their way, no matter what. It's super romantic.

"Sorry," I say pathetically. "It's been a long day—long month, too."

Georgie slides her hand across the table and gives mine a pat. "It's okay. I know this new job hasn't been easy. Sam is just happy you joined the team. He needs people he can trust so he can focus on managing the business side of things."

"Okay. I can't hold it in any longer," says the brunette with thick hipster glasses, wearing a *Nerds are Tasty* shirt. A picture of a box of blue Nerds is doing something inappropriate to a pink box. "I'm Tass. So nice to meet you." She holds out her hand, and we shake.

"Nice to finally meet you, too," I say. "I've heard you're smarter than Elle. Is that true?"

Elle, who's a honey blonde, is wearing jeans and a T-shirt with a picture of a cat that says "Mr. Nucleus II" across the top. "Tass is *not* smarter than me. I've got her by a whole twenty IQ points."

"True," Tass says, "but I've got way more street smarts, and there's no test to measure that other than an apocalypse."

"And if we were in one," Elle argues, "I'd have a new self-sustaining, solar-powered colony up and running in half the time it would take you."

Georgie leans closer to talk to me while Tass and Elle trade statistics on which physical and mental traits would prove more advantageous to survival.

"You're so bad, Abi." Georgie snickers, knowing I sparked the debate on purpose, just to amuse myself.

"I know, but who can resist listening to this?" I love a good geek-off.

"Ha!" Elle throws her hands in the air. "I win! You can't feed a colony of ten thousand people if you live in the desert. The power required to pump groundwater would exceed the output of your solar panels."

"Hmph!" Tass crosses her arms and pushes back into her seat. "Fine. You win. But you have to admit that my idea of solar is far more feasible than traditional power methods if you're looking to automate."

Automate during an apocalypse? I shrug at Georgie, who smiles and pours me a beer from the pitcher. "So, what brings you out to girls' night? Besides the stimulating female company?"

I take my mug, tip it back, and let the cold suds fizz down my throat. "Well," I plunk the drink on the table, "I stopped an old woman from stabbing our client tonight."

"What?" Georgie's back stiffens.

I nod. "Yep."

"How come Sam didn't tell me?" she asks.

I'm guessing because he wouldn't want her to worry. "I'm sure he will. Right now he's tied up making sure the assassin is properly jailed."

"I can't believe it," says Georgie, pushing her wavy brown hair from her face. "How did you catch her?"

I relay the facts about the mud, but leave out the reporter. It feels lame to tell them how easily I was duped by a hot Englishman.

"That's freaking amazing," says Tass. "I'm such a wuss. I'd never be able to throw myself at a hit nana."

"It was luck, really," I reply. "I'm not even supposed to get involved in any of the action. My training went as far as handling a gun, observation, and how to report suspicious people. Hand-to-hand is not my thing."

"But is it true you went *hand-to-hand* with Mitch Hofer, or was it dangly bit to muffin bit?" asks Elle, snorting into her mug of what looks like a soda.

I swivel my head at Georgie. "Seriously? You told them?"

"No...I just mentioned that you may have hooked up with Mitch the night of that party and you both looked adorable together."

"Georgie!" I protest, feeling genuinely pissed. "Why are you gossiping about my personal life?"

Two rotund guys in cowboy boots and saggy jeans walk up and ask if we want to play darts with them.

"Daryl! Thought you'd never ask!" Tass jumps up, likely sensing an argument about to break out between me and Georgie.

"I'm in!" Elle gets up to join them, and the four head across the room near the pool tables.

"Sorry." Georgie leans in. "It's just…I was trying to figure out why Mitch would treat you like he did. It's not like Sam to take on a complete dickhead as a client. Protecting someone is serious stuff."

I give Georgie the death stare.

"What?" she barks. "You can't deny I have a point."

"I don't know what Sam's reasons are. All I know is that Mitch is not a nice man. At least, not to me." He didn't even thank me for saving his life. He just left the room. Afterwards, he ordered me into his limo. Not a thank-you in sight!

"I thought the same thing about Sam at one point. And look how wrong I turned out to be."

"That was different," I argue. "Sam was playing the role of mean boss so you wouldn't catch on to who he really was." Meaning, an undercover FBI agent. "Look. I'm over it. I don't even like Mitch, so it doesn't matter why he did what he did."

She leans in closer to whisper just loud enough so I can hear over the country music now playing on the jukebox. "But why do you think someone wants him dead?"

I shrug. "Ask Sam."

"I did. He won't tell me. Says it's for my own good."

"All I know is that some old lady showed up to the fundraiser, ready to gut Mitch like a fish."

"Maybe he knocked up her granddaughter or something."

No. It feels much bigger than that. Otherwise, why would those reporters be working so hard for information? On the other hand, "Well, Mitch is a global celebrity who can't seem to keep it in his pants," except with me, "so maybe you're right."

"Either way, be careful, Abi. I hate the idea of anything happening to you."

"I'll be fine." Maybe. "Plus, I kind of like the idea of being someone's protector."

"You always were like my personal bodyguard at school."

Yeah. I guess I was. I hated being in the spotlight or drawing attention to myself, but when anyone picked on Georgie, I automatically became this other person. The first time it happened, it was with this boy, Jimmy Wilson. He tripped Georgie in the cafeteria as she walked by with her tray of mac n' cheese. She went flying and so did her lunch. While the room of seventh graders laughed, I turned into a raging bull. I grabbed Jimmy by the collar, yanked him off the bench where he sat with his posse, and slapped him so hard he had a red mark on his cheek for two whole days. When the teacher on duty asked what happened, he didn't dare open his mouth.

Georgie claimed she'd tripped. I think because she knew that getting thrown to the floor and bitch-slapped by a girl was more humiliating for poor little Jimmie than a trip to the principal's office. Either way, that was the day Georgie and I became best friends instead of just two people who hung out at school because we shared the same social name tag: Nerds.

I look at Georgie and smile. "I guess I always have had the protector gene."

"It's more than that, Abi. You feel personally responsible for the people you care about. Really, for anyone in need or neglected. It's why I love you."

"I love you, too." I try my best not to tear up. It's been an emotional day, and I hate crying in public.

"So I have good news! I'm going to Miami with you guys next weekend."

"What?" I lurch forward in my chair. "It's not safe."

She waves a dismissive hand through the air. "I'll be fine. Don't worry."

"Of course I'm worried. What if some crazy sniper shows up and—"

"I'm not going anywhere near Mitch or the events he's attending. I'll be safe and sound back at my swanky hotel a mile away from you guys."

"Yeah, but—"

"But nothing, Abi. I'm a big girl. And I really need this break. The last time I went anywhere, it was to a naked yoga cult as my father's hostage. Exotic, yes. Vacay, no. Plus, this is my last chance to have noisy, hot boyfriend-slash-fiancé sex with Sam before we get married."

Ick. I hate thinking about Sam, my boss, and her humping away. "What about Joy? You can't leave her." I have to find some reason for Georgie to stay home.

"We're locking her in the pantry. She'll be fine." Georgie huffs. "Abi! Come on. You know she'll be with Erin, Sam's sister in-law. Stop worrying and bask in the awesome fact that you and I will get to hit a few clubs, do some shopping, and let loose."

"I'll be working." I cross my arms over my chest.

"Only during the day. Your nights will be free." She crosses her arms in rebuttal.

"Except when I'm on duty because Mitch decides to hit a party."

She throws back, "Then we'll hang when you're off the next morning. Breakfast. A run on the beach. Stop arguing, or I'll start thinking you don't want to spend time with me."

"Insanity! I just have a bad feeling about whatever is going on with Mitch."

"You think Sam would let me go to Miami if he felt I'd be in harm's way?"

"No. But you could've used your feminine trickeries on him. Offered him a blow job or something so he'd let you go with us."

"Abi!"

I eye her critically.

She rolls her eyes. "Fine. Yes. I did! But then you're insinuating that he values a good sucky-sucky over my life, and I promise you I'm not that good at it."

"Sucky-sucky?"

Georgie blushes. "I don't like the word *blow job*. Okay? I mean, really. Is there any blowing involved at all? And if you're really into a guy, it's not a job. It's fun."

"Sucky-sucky sounds like a term from some weird foreign porn." I try not to crack up. "Couldn't you use a more mature phrase like smoking the pole or knob gobbling?"

"Stop making fun of me." She stifles a grin. "Or I'll kick you in the woman balls."

I hold my hands up in surrender. "I'm done."

"Good. Because I can't wait to go to Miami with you for a little M & M."

"You mean R & R."

"Nope. M & M. Mischief and mayhem."

I hang my head. "No, Georgie. No to both. If I get any downtime, I need peace and quiet. Maybe a poolside massage, a bubble bath, some serious Netflix time."

She smiles with that sneaky grin of hers, which sets off alarm bells. "Yes to all of those." She takes a tiny sip of beer, makes a sour face, and sets the mug back down. "This tastes funny."

She's trying to change the subject. "Georgie…" I growl in warning.

"I promise. Every free second you have will be utterly and totally dedicated to relaxation."

"I don't believe you."

"I know. But what choice do you have now? I'm coming with you to Miami, and your boss is my fiancé, so you just have to suck it up like a big ol' Hoover."

"I hate you with my eyes." I glare at her.

"And I love you with my heart. So, wanna ride the mechanical bull?"

"I thought it was broken?" I say.

"It was. Now it's fixed and ready for your sorry ass."

I raise my brows. It's funny how Georgie is the shyer one, but somehow always manages to push me outside my comfort zone. It's what I love about her. "Sure, but I'll have to do it sidesaddle." I point down to the hem on my super-short dress.

"I'd pay money to watch that." She laughs. "I'm sure a bunch of the men here would too. Wanna see?"

I'm game for new experiences. And who doesn't have sidesaddling a mechanical bull on their bucket list? "Let's ride."

CHAPTER TEN

When I pull up to my house in the Uber, only slightly bruised on my ass from the three-second bull challenge, I'm comforted by the lights turned off inside and my mother's van in the driveway. She's safe, sound, and asleep.

I thank the driver and slip from the car, immediately going for my flashlight app. By now, my mom has locked up the house, so I'll need to grab the key from around back.

"Abi," hisses a male voice from the direction of the hedges.

"What the!" I swivel my head and jump back, fumbling with my purse to get to my weapon.

"It's me. Leland." A tall shadow emerges from the hedges.

"What the hell are you doing here?"

He approaches with his hands raised. "I just wanted to be sure you were all right, love."

"Don't you 'all right, love' me, you big fat liar. And how do you know where I live?"

He drops his hands. "I am a reporter; it's my job

to find information. And my sincerest apologies for the ruse, but I meant no harm. I merely wished to—"

"Lie to me? Make me think you're someone you're not so I'd give you information you're not entitled to?"

"Well, yes. But that doesn't mean I wished you harm. I simply want the truth."

Grrrr... "Well, then, you won't mind hearing my version of it."

"Not at all, love." He pulls a recording device from his coat pocket.

Ass! "The truth is that you have no clue what you're messing with. But when you publicly single out someone like me, someone who is supposed to stay in the shadows, being a lookout, you expose me. And that," I poke his chest, "means you are placing someone's life in jeopardy. Mine. Yours. The client we protect. And everyone around us."

"So you're saying Mitch Hofer is in danger. Do you know any details? When the next attempt on his life might be? Who's behind it?"

Ohmygod. "You're missing the point. You're also an asshole. That's what I'm saying. And if I ever see you within a hundred yards of me or anyone I know, I'll personally get a restraining order."

He chuckles. "Good luck with that, dove. Freedom of the press and all."

"Leave. Now. Because I have a gun in my purse, and I'm not afraid to shoot a nut with it. It's a mini pistol, so I'm fairly sure it's the perfect size for such a small job."

I expect this douche to leave, but instead he steps closer. "Abi, do you even know why you're guarding a world-famous swimmer? Do you know what he's really involved with? Because if you did, I doubt you'd be putting your sweet arse on the line for him."

Hmmm... All right. I'll bite. "Why don't you tell me what you know, and I'll confirm yes or no."

He wags a finger in front of my nose. "Nuh-uh-uh..." he chants. "My information comes with a price. You help me, and I'll tell you what I know."

"But you don't know anything. You're full of shit—a fact we've already established on this fine evening."

"Have we now?" His tone is pompous yet playful, like he actually thinks this is some big game.

It's not. Which is why I really want to know what he knows. "Give me one good reason to believe that you have any information of value or deserve my trust."

"Mitch Hofer is a witness to a murder being investigated by the International Court of Justice."

I laugh. "Are Aquaman and Wonder Woman helping out?"

"Laugh all you like, Abi, but the war criminals who go on trial there do not."

Oh. That international court. "You're serious."

"Yes."

"What war crimes are we talking about?"

Leland smiles. "I'll scratch your back if you scratch mine."

I stop to think before responding. If what Leland says is true, then the threat against Mitch is much deadlier and much uglier than I thought.

Damn that Sam! I want a raise. And yes, maybe a tiny part of me, buried deep down inside, underneath my secret desires for Santa to be real, that tossing coins into fountains really does grant wishes, and food in liquid forms doesn't actually count, there's a whimper of concern for Mitch. I may detest the man, but I don't want him dead. *Shhh… Tell no one.*

"Fine." I huff. "What do you want to know?"

"Where you'll be. When. With whom."

"How do I know you won't feed that information to Mitch's would-be killers?"

"Because I was there the day this all started, thinking it was just another assignment—spying on a celebrity for an exposé."

"I'm sorry. Did you just say you're a witness, too?"

"Yes. And no one can know. Not ever. But the faster I can expose the people behind everything and have them put away, the safer we all are."

"And the woman who showed up at the party—the one you were whisper fighting with?"

"She's a mistake. Someone I never should have trusted."

I've been there before.

"So we have a deal?" he asks.

I give it a moment of thought. Obviously, he could be full of complete BS. *Which is why I could tell him some information, something that was already public knowledge so there's no harm in sharing.* It would give me time to validate whatever he tells me. Once trust is established, we'll see what comes next.

"Yes. We have a deal," I say. "Now tell me what you know."

MITCH

It's almost midnight when I hear the doorbell. I freeze on my padded plank, where I've been doing inverted sit-ups for the last twenty minutes. This weekend is the big swimsuit fashion show in Miami, and my sponsors don't pay me to have a one-pack.

Which you'll be getting if you don't back off the empty carbs—my all-time favorite food. I know the category isn't a food. Not specifically. But a guy like me doesn't discriminate—white bread, cookies, donuts, candy—I dream about them all. Lately I've been so damned stressed out that I've been falling into old patterns. Yeah. That was me, the kid who looked like a giant beach ball. It was the reason my uncle, who was also my guardian, put me into swimming. At first, I hated the sport because, let's face it, no boy wants to wear those damned salami hammocks if they've got a spare tire. Or two. Ankle biters at that age are monsters. But after a few days, I realized that when I was in the pool, no one could really see me. I spent as much time as possible in the water—first to arrive to practice and the last to leave so fewer people would see me. A few months later, that baby fat began turning into muscle. Puberty kicked in and the rest is history. I got taller, leaner, and most important, faster. I can't say I've ever struggled with weight since I exercise year-round, but my body doesn't perform if I feed it crap.

I glance longingly at my giant Italian sub with extra cheese and cold cuts, waiting for me on the little side table near the door of my workout room. *Don't go anywhere. Mitch loves you.*

I get up, go for my cell, and tap the app to view my front porch. Whoever's here was likely let through the gate by one of the two blokes patrolling outside, but can't be too careful these days, especially since those evil bastards are after me.

The brown hair and agitated movements are immediately recognizable. *Abi. Why's she here?*

I pull on my gray T-shirt and go to let her in since my indoor staff is gone for the day. When I open the door, Abi pushes past me, yelling so fast, I can't understand more than a few bits and pieces. I surmise she's found out more than she should.

"Why, Mitch? Why did you refuse to go into witness protection?" She plants her hands on her waist. "Do you have any idea what's going to happen to you?"

"They'll kill me?" I wrap an invisible rope around my neck and pull up.

"Ohmygod! Do not joke at a time like this." She shoves a finger in my face. "You don't fuck around with people like that."

I notice that she's still wearing her short purple dress underneath her partially unbuttoned black coat. Does she have any idea how distracting she is when just in normal clothes? But this dress... *So damned sexy.* I have to wonder if she's doing this on purpose—her way of punishing me for the way I treated her. First the dress, then throwing herself at that guy during my fundraiser. She wants me to suffer and see what I'm missing.

"Who said I'm fucking around?"

"Mitch." She grabs my hand, which throws me off. It reminds me of that night. Her touch did things to me. Dirty, exciting things. Right now, it's reminding me how hard I wanted to fuck her.

She goes on, oblivious to my true feelings. "It's not a question of if. It's a question of when they get to you. You have to run. You have to go into hiding."

"You've been talking to Sam." I close the front door and lock it before heading back to my workout room, where that sandwich is calling my name.

With all this damned stress, I need something not on my regular diet, which is high calorie but no fun: lean organic meats, organic fruits and vegetables, lots of healthy fats—like avocados and raw nuts—and tons of slow-burning complex carbs. The shit I crave, like cookies and French bread, sabotages my swimming. Sugar crashes are the enemy when you're training and trying to maintain muscle mass.

"No," she says, following on my heels. "I have not been talking to Sam."

"Then how did you find out?" I grab my sandwich and head for the kitchen to find a cold brew to go with my snack. She can yell at me all she wants, just as long as she lets me eat. This sub has extra mayo and bacon, too. *If I could inject it into my veins, I would.*

"The how doesn't matter," she replies. "What does is the fact you're insane if you stay here or go to Miami or anywhere public for that matter."

I sit at the breakfast bar in my large chef's kitchen with top-of-the-line appliances and two of everything. The house was built for entertaining, but I bought it because it was also built to keep people out. The guy who used to own it was some sort of money launderer. Sam told me about the place after the feds seized it.

I pick up my guilty pleasure with both hands. "I'm not going to give up everything I've worked for just because a bunch of rich thugs are after me." I open my mouth and go in for a big bite, only to have the entire sandwich swatted from my grasp.

"They're not some group of petty criminals from Podunk!" Abi yells. "These are powerful people. And you're a witness to a murder they arranged. Your uncle's murder."

"Hey!" I turn my head and snarl. "That was my sandwich!"

She takes her spiked black heel and stomps on the thing, grinding it into the floor. "Not anymore. And how can you be thinking about your stomach at a time like this? Someone tried to stab you tonight. Your uncle is dead."

She thinks I don't know that? I watched him get gunned down in broad daylight right outside our house back in Sydney. All because he had some old WWII photos he intended to give away to a local war museum. Albert, my uncle, had no clue what the photos were. He thought they were part of a large collection belonging to my grandfather George—God rest his soul. He obtained them during his time as a war photographer in the 1940s. It turns out the photos were evidence thought to have been buried long ago.

"Abi, you should leave. And then keep going. Away from me."

She folds her arms across her chest, and I try not to notice her breasts swelling beneath the deep V of her dress. *Damn. I love her breasts.* They're round and firm. Not too big and just enough to play with during—

"Ha! Fat chance, Mitch. If you're not running, why should I?"

"Because I made my choice, and it's my problem. *You* can walk away."

"You think I took this job so I could quit at the first sign of danger?"

"If you were smart, you would." I get up and go to my fridge. I'll have to make another sandwich, but it won't be nearly as delicious as the one she so cruelly murdered from my new favorite sub shop. *Poor sandwich...it will never know its home: the inside of my stomach.*

"What are you doing?" she gripes while I go for my boring whole-grain bread, turkey slices, and low-fat cheese.

"What does it look like. I'm hungry."

"Ugh. Such an ass."

"Would you like one?" I offer. She looks hungry, too, but maybe that's because she's much thinner than when we first met. Back then, she was a bit curvier and fuller in the hips. Very sexy. Now she's got these tiny muscles in her biceps, and her stomach is flatter than mine. Sam mentioned this bootcamp he sends his team to is tough, but I'm guessing he didn't tell me how tough. Regardless, I like this version of Abi, too.

"I'm starving. Thanks," she says, "but don't change the subject."

"Can't help it if you want to talk about the wrong topic." I grab two plates and a butter knife from the utensil drawer. "Which is the fact that you should leave here and never look back. Finish your degree, live your life, be happy. Don't get mixed up in this shit for a paycheck. It's not worth it."

In fact, why don't I just write her a check. I set down my knife and go to my home office just down the hallway, returning a moment later with my checkbook.

"What are you doing?" Abi's golden brown eyes look like they're about to bolt from her skull and accost me.

Well, too bad. I'm doing this. "Will twenty thousand do the trick?" I start filling out the check.

She swats my arm again, and the pen goes flying.

"You're getting on my last nerve, woman."

"My name is Abi, not woman. And you think you can throw money at me, and I'll give up?"

"You see me writing a check, don't you?"

Her tiny nostrils flare. "I don't take charity. And I don't quit." She lifts her chin defiantly, and fuck me, but she looks so damned hot. It may have something to do with the fact that I'm not a quitter either.

Don't care. Don't want her. She needs to stop this game of pretending to be a bodyguard. A) She has almost no training. B) How can someone smaller than me protect my life?

You mean like she did tonight? I argue with myself.

It was luck. Plain luck, I counter.

I throw my hands in the air. "And what are you going to do, eh, when some bloke shows up with a magazine full of bullets that have my name on them?"

"Well—well..."

"You can't do anything. Which is why I've already told Sam that you either stay put here, or I'm cancelling his services." I stand tall and hover over her. It's not lost on me that I enjoy this position.

No. Not her. Not anyone. My days of being a player are long gone, even if I still have my entourage, who are paid by my swimsuit sponsor's PR company. It's an image thing the sponsor demanded. The ladies are to accompany me to any publicity events for Weeno, "*The swimsuit for real men with real substance.*"

Wankers. Why don't they just call them "Hey, I'm a shallow prick." The irony is that they sell the bathing suits—or swimmers, as I like to call them back home—with a special insert to make the guy's cock look bigger, so if anyone sees you wearing a Weeno, they automatically think you've got a shrimp in your shorts.

Once my contract is over after the fashion show, I'm done. I'll sign on with someone more respectable, like Wheaties or something. My body wasn't put on this earth to be a marketing *tool.* I'm an athlete. I have four gold medals. I've broken five world records. Yeah, sure, it's nice not having a micro-penis, so you'd never catch me complaining about my big cock, but this whole "Bulge" thing is out of control. I never asked for the attention to my downstairs, and I can't help it if I have to wear a uniform that gives me the appearance of showing off. On my regular days, when I hang at the beach with my mates, I wear board shorts like a normal guy.

Of course, my normal days are over. Being around me is dangerous. I've already told Weeno that my entourage can't come to this final event. It's one thing for them to show up to a small TV studio or closed photo shoot, but the Miami Swimsuit Fashion Week is bloody chaos. There are thousands of people everywhere, security is flimsy, and Sam's made it clear he can't guarantee my safety. No one can, which is why he doesn't want me to go.

I look at Abi. "You can't come to Miami with us. I won't allow it."

"Mitch." Abi grabs my right hand. The subtle note of genuine concern in her eyes makes me want to give in to her. "I can at least be there to tell you to duck or run or do something. If I go, your odds of survival dramatically increase, and isn't that what your family would want?"

I have very few family left. My grandparents are dead. My father and mother passed before I was ten. My uncle, who raised me, died last year. All I have now are a few distant cousins, one who lives here in Houston. I barely know him, but I'm trying to change that.

"It won't be enough." I go back to making sandwiches. *Who can think on an empty stomach?*

"Then answer this question for me, Mitch. Do

you want the people who murdered your uncle to get off free? Do you think they have the right to take your life?"

"You know I don't think that."

"Well, neither do I, because if it were my uncle they'd hurt, I'd be pissed as hell. They don't get to bury the shame of their family because of greed. They don't get to commit murder and rob you of someone you loved. Which means you have to stay alive and testify."

I agree, but I'd add the point that they don't get to rob me of a second chance at competing in the Olympics either. Swimming is my life, and I've sacrificed more than anyone knows.

And there's no fucking way I'll let these greedy bastards walk. They've already caught the guy who killed my uncle. He goes by the name of Kristoff Bones and is a ruthless piece of garbage, though it's hard to take him seriously with a name like that. Bones makes me think of *Star Trek*, one of my all-time favorite shows. Either way, Kristoff's the one who put an open hit on me since he's in prison and can't get the job done himself. He's not talking to authorities about who hired him, but I know. The Kemmler family's behind it, which is why Interpol is working with local authorities to issue warrants in Germany and Switzerland.

The sticky part of this is that everything hinges on those warrants. If they find no connection to Kristoff or he doesn't cave and cooperate, the

Kemmler family will get off free.

So why do they want me dead?

Two reasons: One, I witnessed my uncle's murder. When Kristoff finally goes on trial, my testimony puts him away for life.

Two, it's a well-known fact that I have a photographic memory—a result of world-class coaching techniques focusing heavily on recall. I have almost as many hours in the pool as I have outside, visualizing the strokes of my arms and feeling my legs kick at just the right thrust to put me across the finish line faster than anyone else.

My memory is why they're afraid I might've seen the black-and-white photos before my uncle was killed. *And they're right.* I see them now just as clearly as if I were holding them in my hand. They show Nazi soldiers standing next to a snow-covered embankment next to the River Meuse in Dinant, Belgium, while saluting a man. To someone like my uncle, and even to myself at the time before I became interested in this specific topic, they look like any other wartime photos. A bloody moment of history that would live on in books, movies, and even video games. But to the family of the man being saluted, they are proof of a legacy they wanted to erase forever. To them, the photos show Ralf Kemmler was in command—a junior officer promoted on the battlefield after their unit suffered considerable casualties. The pictures prove he was there, and being that he was in command, he was the only person who could have given the order to execute a group of British Allied soldiers after they were captured near Dinant. Under the Geneva Convention, prisoners of war are supposed to be provided shelter, food, and medical attention. But food was scarce. The weather was grueling and cold. They were losing. Ralf Kemmler decided it was better to murder the men even though the plan of attack had failed. They were about to lose the war.

Later, after the war ended, Kemmler was set free. There was no firm evidence to disprove his claims—that he was nothing more than a foot soldier, as his official papers stated, and he played no part in the executions. At the time, my grandfather's photos weren't known about, and after he passed, his belongings were packed in boxes and stored in my uncle's attic.

Then, one day, my uncle is cleaning out our attic, and he finds the box. Thinking these are pieces of history belonging in a museum, he scans part of the collection and posts them on a few historian chat groups specifically dedicated to this particularly infamous battle. The next thing I know, the pictures disappear from those sites, my uncle is lying facedown in the driveway, and there's a man pulling away in a gray van just as I'm coming back from a run.

I got a good look at the asshole and the car. The stroke of luck was that the police happened to be two blocks over, dealing with some other issue.

Kristoff Bones was caught later that morning after a long car chase, but no one knows what happened to the photos.

So why do I assume Albert was killed over all this when Ralf Kemmler has been dead for years? Money.

After the war, Ralf Kemmler ended up founding the world's biggest greeting-card company with a presence in twenty-two countries. And even though the family doesn't have any direct ties to this dark chapter of history, nobody wants to buy birthday cards from people associated with a mass-murderer Nazi. If these photos get out, or if I publicly identify Ralf Kemmler as the person I saw being saluted, it would sink a three-hundred-million-euro company.

I still wonder how the family heard about the photos at all. Maybe the family keeps an eye out for stuff. Maybe they have connections in some of the museums my uncle approached.

Doesn't matter. Because they messed with the wrong Aussie. I might run around in swimmers and pose in fashion magazines, but that's not a pussy I'm packing down there. Not that there's anything wrong with those. I damned well love 'em.

"Abi," I draw a breath, "I'm not going to let these massive wankers ruin my career and get away with murder. But you, woman, are just another liability, so why don't you leave the bodyguarding to the pros, eh?"

Her face turns a fiery shade of red. "If I weren't

so determined to make you eat those sexist words, I'd kill you myself. That, and I think it's really awful what they did."

She's sweet. Too damned sweet. But I can't call myself a man, knowing she's absolutely, most definitely going to get hurt if she stays with this job.

They are coming for me.

They won't stop.

But I chose not to go into hiding, and I am not a guy worth dying for. I'm just a regular bloke who loves swimming. But I'm no one worth kicking the bucket over. Sam, Phil, and the other guys are ex-soldiers, and they've seen it all. They know what they're getting into. But Abi is a nice girl. The type us men live to fight for, not the other way around.

"Sweetheart, take the money. You can't be a bodyguard. You can't be anything but hot."

Her small hand whips across my face with a hard slap. "Fuck you, Mitch."

I really wish she wouldn't use that word. *Fuck.* It makes me think of what I want to do to her right now. I'd also like to tell her that no one has the right to dictate what she does, so she's right to give me a wallop, but I want her gone. By any means possible.

"Naw, Abi. If I wanted a screw, I would've done it the night you begged me to."

She narrows those eyes. "You're disgusting."

"Basically, yeah." *Don't you understand that I'm not worth your life? Just leave, woman. Leave.*

And she does, but it's not without some guilt on

my part. I take no pleasure in treating her like this.

Be strong. You know what's right.

"And don't come back!" I yell.

CHAPTER ELEVEN

ABI

"What an ass! If he wants me to quit, then fine, I'll quit," I mumble as I walk to the front gate and let myself out. I hit my Uber app and see it's a six-minute wait, so I decide to text Sam.

Me: *You up? We need to talk.*

No reply. "Come on. Answer."

Me: *???*

Sam: *. . .*

My phone rings, and it's him. "Hello?"

"Why are you at Mitch's house at twelve thirty at night?"

"How do you know where I am?" The night air is cold, so I start buttoning my coat with one shivering hand. The street Mitch lives on is quiet, but well lit. It's the kind of neighborhood where the homes are big and people are overly paranoid, so I feel fairly safe.

Other than a bunch of crazy hit men on the loose, possibly watching Mitch's house. I pat my purse, ensuring I've come prepared.

"You're using the company phone. We have trackers on them. Didn't Cray tell you?"

"No. But that's spying."

"It's safety. What if you're kidnapped or something?"

"Oh. That. Okay, fine, it's appropriate," I reluctantly admit.

"What's not is you being at the client's house so late when you're not working."

"Well, it won't be a problem again, because I quit, Sam. Mitch is a complete turd-kabob. Like, not just one turd, but a whole string of nastiness all stuck together in one giant shitty mess."

Sam is silent at first, which makes me think he's preparing his argument.

"I agree," he says.

"Sorry?"

"I agree. This was a mistake. I never should have hired you."

Huh? "Is this some reverse psychology thing?"

"Nope. It's me admitting I was wrong. I knew Mitch would resist having you in his detail. I knew you two had some sort of falling-out."

"We never fell in. So it's a little hard to fall out."

"The details don't concern me," he says. "This situation is dangerous, and I should've known better."

"Yeah, I heard about the war photos and Mitch's uncle."

"So he told you." Sam sighs.

"Not exactly. That reporter came to my house. He wanted information—said he'd scratch my back if I scratched his."

"Dammit. That guy is relentless. I'm almost tempted to leak the story to his competitor Gisselle just so they'll go away."

Gisselle is the woman who showed up to the charity event and started fighting with Leland.

"So, Sam, what's the plan?"

"What do you mean?" he asks.

"When does Mitch testify? When does all this end?" Because first he's got to make it alive until this Kristoff guy's trial. Then it sounds like this international court is investigating the Kemmler family's part in the murder and whether or not it's tied to those photos. Leland sounded convinced. So did Mitch. I just wonder if Mitch telling this court what he saw in the pictures is enough to bring the Kemmlers to justice. I'm no lawyer, but it sounds flimsy. Regardless, what I think doesn't matter. If the Kemmlers want history buried, they'll bury it.

"I really don't know when this will be over," Sam says; his voice sounds deeply troubled. "Everything's being handled in closed court sessions. My job is just to keep Mitch safe until he's summoned."

I suddenly feel bad for quitting like this. "Are you going to be all right? I mean, do you have enough people to cover Mitch in Miami?"

"I could have a hundred people surrounding him at all times, and it wouldn't be enough. He shouldn't be going at all."

Well, great! Now I feel like the turd-kabob.

Sam adds, "The people behind this basically placed an ad in Craigslist for assassins. One million dollars in cryptocurrency to anyone who kills Mitch."

"Jesus, even I'd consider killing him for that much money."

"Not funny, Abi. It's going to take a miracle to keep him alive. It was a mistake even taking him on as a client—the man needs an army, not body-guards."

"Why did you agree to protect him, then?"

"His uncle was a close friend of mine back when I was in the Marines. He was part of a training exchange with the Australians. They hosted several survivalist bootcamps in the outback."

"Oh. I'm so sorry. I didn't know you were friends." But it explains why Sam has been so over-the-top hands-on when he's supposed to be letting Phil handle everything.

"Albert called me right before he was murdered. He said he thought someone was watching the house. He asked me to look after Mitch if anything happened."

My heart sinks. "He should've gone into hid-ing."

"I was the one who talked him out of it."

"What! Why?" I bark.

"Albert, his uncle, was Mitch's biggest fan. He cashed in his retirement to hire coaches and pay for travel to all of Mitch's first competitions. Watching him swim was probably Albert's biggest joy in life, and I think if he knew Mitch quit when he was at the pinnacle of his career, all because of these corrupt, greedy assholes, well..."

"It would break his heart. I get that. But his uncle is gone. Mitch isn't."

"Trust me, I know I made a mistake. I've admitted it to Mitch, but now he won't listen."

"This is the stupidest situation ever," I mutter to myself.

"Now I have no choice but to do my best and help Mitch come out of this alive. With or without me, he's going to Miami."

Don't do it, Abi. Don't say it. Resist...need...to...help... Dammit, me! "I changed my mind. I'm coming, too."

"No, Abi, you're not."

"I *want* to come. Not for him but for you." I can't even imagine how Sam is going to feel if anything happens to Mitch. And whatever happens to Sam happens to Georgie and happens to me. Kind of like a really fucked up three musketeers. "Besides, Georgie invited me to hang out, so I'm going to be there regardless."

"I don't think it's the best idea. I can't afford

the distraction of you and Mitch fighting."

"He won't even know I'm there. I'll stay away completely—in the back of the room, at the back of the crowd, wearing a wig so not even he recognizes me."

Sam is silent for a long moment. "Okay. But I'm only agreeing because I could use an extra set of eyes lurking in the shadows."

"Hoo hoo," I hoot like an owl.

"Come to the office around noon tomorrow. We have a team meeting to prepare."

Just then my Uber pulls up. "See you there." I end the call, and the moment I slide inside the car, it dawns on me. "Sonofabitch! He totally mind fucked me into going to Miami." I laugh and shake my head. "He's good. He's really, really good." Either way, my reason for going is the right one. I now see that this isn't just about Mitch's life anymore. It's about a whole lot more, so if Mitch doesn't like having a chick bodyguard, well, too damned bad.

CHAPTER TWELVE

The next morning, I spend time hanging out with my mom and catching up on major chores, like laundry. Normally, I look forward to our time together. We laugh, we talk about her eccentric clients, and I tell her about whatever super-cheesy romance book I'm hooked on. But now, I just feel guilty about all of the lies, and I think she senses it. Every time we're in the same room, she's drilling me about the new job or why I look so stressed out.

"I'm fine, Mom. Stop asking, okay?"

The wounded look in her eyes was instant and now we're not talking.

Fuck. This is such a mess. I hit the buzzer on the door of Sam's offices, and Cray greets me with a bear hug. "That's mi girl!"

"What…errr…" I grunt under the extreme pressure of his tight grip. "What did I do to deserve that welcome?"

He releases me, but grabs my shoulders firmly. "I knew ye wouldn't abandon your team. I told Sam not teh bet against ye."

"Bet? Seriously?"

He slaps my arm. "Won me a hundred." He trots off in the direction of the conference room.

These guys are placing bets on me? They seriously need a kick in the knickers.

When I finally catch up, I find Phil, Igor, and four other men who look like the most stylish, adorable boy band ever all sitting around the conference room table.

Oh! Sam's smart. The boy band will blend in perfectly at the fashion event. Another guy, who looks insanely pale with biceps the size of watermelons, is sitting in the corner, eyeing everyone suspiciously.

Oh, and we have an albino Hulk. We're just like the Avengers now. Only our superpowers are less exciting—good dressers, extreme antisocialism, and wallflower power. That last one is me. I've had extensive experience in the fine art of not drawing attention to myself, a leftover from my Blabi days.

I take the seat next to Phil, who's in a suit as usual. I'm guessing he's got Mitch duty later.

Sam enters the room, wearing jeans and a black tee, with a purposeful stride. He stands at the head of the table like a drill sergeant.

"All right, everyone," Sam says. "Thanks for coming. As you know, this weekend in Miami is going to be extremely challenging." Sam pulls a clicker thing from his pocket and steps aside. A projector suspended from the ceiling pops on and displays a map on the white wall in front of us. He goes over the first stop in the morning, which is a Weeno breakfast and photo op for their clients, mostly buyers from the large department stores. In the afternoon is a photo shoot. In the evening is the big to-do Weeno swimwear show followed by the after-party.

I try not to laugh every time Sam says Weeno. I think it's supposed to be like Speedo for the well-endowed man, but it just sounds ridiculous. Like, "*We know*...you have a tiny one." On the other hand, women do pad their bras all the time. No, we don't call our bras lame names like Mount Boob-More, Chia Tits, or Tah-tah-tastic, or whatever, but I shouldn't judge men for wanting to make a *big* impression at the beach.

"Any questions?" Sam asks and starts handing out packets containing floor plans for the three venues of the day.

I raise my hand. "What if I see that Leland guy? Do I treat him as friend or foe?"

"He's not our focus. So unless he's getting in your way, ignore him."

Easy enough. I mean, yeah, he's smokin' hot, but now that I know he was only flirting with me to get info, his gorgeous smile has lost its shine.

I nod. "And any tips on what we should be looking out for besides the usual?" Suspicious vibe. Carnivorous staring. *Touching one's self inappropriately while standing next to Mitch.*

"The events have their own security," Sam replies, "so our focus will be on the crowd when Mitch is traveling from his hotel suite to the conference center or walking from one room to another."

"But won't the bad guy, gal, granny, grampa, toddler assassin know that?" I shrug. "I mean, if it were me, and I really wanted to kill Mitch, which I don't—though I have thought about it—I would be trying to get to him when everyone's guard is down."

"Or you just assume no one is safe," grumbles snowflake Hulk. "Nothing is safe. Everyone has a grenade in their pants." His eyes go vacant like he's imagining lots and lots of people with grenades. In their pants.

"Well, that wasn't weird," I mumble.

Cray speaks up with his thick brogue. "Let me know if anyone would like to take some of mi special whiskey and Red Bull elixir to steady their nerves and alert their minds…"

Sam gives him a look. "No drinking. No caffeine. Definitely not both together. It will make you have to use the restroom, and we need to be in camel mode."

"Only tryin' to help." Cray sticks out his lower lip.

Sam jumps straight into our positions and roles for each room, including our wardrobe changes. "Cray has everything ready for you, so don't forget to grab your outfits on the way out."

"Wait. Why am I going to be dressed in a gross brown jumpsuit?" I ask, staring down at my assignment sheet. It details everything I need to memorize before departure.

Sam's response comes with a stern warning in his tone. "You've been assigned the rolling trash can, so what else would you wear?"

"You mean I'm actually going to be picking up garbage? In Miami. At a glamorous fashion event."

"Yes."

I narrow my eyes.

Sam replies flatly, "I picked you because you're the only one on the team who wouldn't rouse suspicion working in maintenance."

I look around at the beefcakes and pretty boys around the table. "Fine. But I still think it's super un-PC."

"As opposed to dressing like a hooker who's part of Mr. Hofer's harem, and having to let me grab your ass as part of your cover?" Phil retorts and makes a sour face.

"Stop. I know you enjoyed it, but point taken." After all, this is the job. We don't dictate societal norms. We're not here to teach lessons or make political statements. We're supposed to blend in with what is. If we're at the opera with the Queen of England, we curtsy and raise our pinkies. If we're at the monster truck show, we pump our fists, scratch our nuts, and drink beer. Or pretend to. *And if we go to Miami's swimsuit fashion week, I dress like a janitor.*

"And I'm totally fine with my cover. Cleaning is an honest living." My grandma was a housekeeper and worked part-time cleaning the elementary school.

"Good. Then see you all on Saturday morning at the event—I'll be arriving late Friday after most of you. Cray will give you your hotel assignments. And since some of you will be traveling with Mitch and leaving early, be sure to tell us now if you need any supplies." Sam looks at the rock-hard Stay Puft dude. "Work related, Chuck."

"I need my protein drinks, man."

"Noted. But yours contain illegal substances, which I cannot help you with."

I crinkle my nose. Seems like Sam must really be in a pinch if he's using this guy. I'm guessing that the rest of his crew is assigned to other clients. Otherwise, Sam wouldn't be going himself.

Actually, he would be. He feels personally obligated to see this through with a positive outcome.

As for me, I'm beginning to feel nervous about this trip. Because if both Mitch and Sam are calling it a suicide mission, then for a newbie like me, it's…it's…well, I don't know what's worse, but it's bad.

Miami. Here I come?

CHAPTER THIRTEEN

MITCH

"What the hell, Sam! I told you I didn't want Abi on this trip. Why did you convince her?" I snarl into my cell as the limo pulls up to the posh hotel smack in the middle of Miami Beach. I don't think it's a coincidence that Sam waited until I'm already here to break the news.

"She volunteered, Mitch. She insisted."

"What did you say? Because it must've been something." I'd gotten her to quit. I'd finally driven her away.

"Don't ask me. I told her it was a mistake asking her to protect you because your life isn't worth saving."

"Har bloody har. You're a fucking riot, mate. But this is no time for jokes. She can't be a part of this."

"Then change your mind. Go home. I can get you on a flight back to Houston at noon."

If I did that, I'd get sued for millions instead of receiving my final paycheck. And the last thing I need is more headaches. My focus needs to be on swimming and winning. "I'm not breaching my contract with Weeno, I'm not going to hide like a coward, and I'm not altering one single day of my life for those greedy Kemmler bastards."

"Then at this point, we need to stick to the plan. And I need Abi. She's the only one who can blend into the crowd or look like one of your Weeno girls if I need her to. By the way, for the record, I really hate saying Weeno girls. It makes me feel dirty."

"Join the club. Which is why after this weekend and my contract is fulfilled, I'm done with them." And, hopefully soon, I'll be given the date to testify against Kristoff. As for the Kemmlers, I've given that cluster of a situation a lot of thought. I have one and only one option to get them to back down, but it's a risk.

"I just hope whatever this sponsor is paying you is worth it," Sam says.

"It is." But on the inside, I know that's a lie. There is no amount of money worth someone getting hurt. "What I meant to say was it's worth it for me. Which is why I'm firing you, Sam. Call back the guys who came with me. Send them home." As I speak, I look directly at the two men who flew in with me, now sitting in the back of the limo. They're dressed like a boy band. I have no idea why.

"Excuse me?" Sam grumbles through the phone.

"I'm terminating your services. I thought I

could justify having your team on this trip since you're all ex-commandos, but that's the asshole I used to be who's speaking. This new asshole couldn't live with himself if anyone got hurt. Especially you." Sam is about to get married. He's got a little monkey at home. He's a good man.

"Is this because Abi is coming?"

Yes. And no. "I meant what I said. Your services are no longer needed, mate." The hotel valet opens the passenger-side door. I draw a deep breath, taking in the winter Miami weather, which is seventy degrees. More like home.

Three women in Hawaiian skirts rush to my limo, holding out floral necklaces. "I gotta go. I'm about to get lei'd."

"If you die, there'll be no one to testify, Mitch! Kristoff goes free! Stay in your room! Don't go outside!" Sam yells through the phone.

Fuck that. My old mate Ash is meeting up with me at a bar just down the street for some pints. He just happens to be in town for business, and I'm not about to miss the opportunity to see him after all these years.

Of course, I've got a disguise. I'm not stupid. And no one is dying for me. My life isn't worth more than someone else's just because I'm famous.

I say goodbye to my bodyguards in the limo, grab my stuff, and prepare to take my chances. Alone.

ABI

"He did *what*? And he's already in Miami?" This is a disaster, and I know it's because of me. *That arrogant, selfish prick!* He'd rather die than let a woman guard him? "I swear, Sam, I'm going to make sure that fucker lives so I can tie him up in my basement and spank some sense into him." Not that I have a basement, but if I did…spanking time! "Please tell me you're not calling back the boy band and you're still going on the trip."

Silence.

"Sam? You are still getting on a plane, aren't you?"

"I can't, Abi. Mitch sent in the termination notice."

"So?"

"If we're not under contract, we can't get into any of the events."

"Again…so? Show up anyway!"

Sam is slow to respond. "Mitch says he'll take out a restraining order against me and my company if we get anywhere near him. I can't afford that kind of bad PR. Not from a celebrity. Definitely not from an ex-client."

That sneaky bastard. "Well, I quit. Again. Now I don't work for you, so I can go."

"Abi, don't. If something happens, we won't be there to help you."

"What about Mitch? Who's going to help him?"

"I hate to say this, but our chances of keeping him safe were low to start. Without his complete cooperation, it's zero. And I'm responsible for my people's safety. I have a four-year-old daughter. I have Georgie."

And I have my mother. She needs me more now than ever, and I'm not talking about the money to save our house and her business. I'm all she's got left of my father. But can I really let Mitch go on a suicide mission?

Sam adds, "I have to draw the line somewhere, Abi. Mitch forced my hand."

I sigh. I know he's right. "I understand. But seriously, I can't help feeling like this is my fault."

"It's not," Sam says firmly. "Mitch is a grown man. He makes his own decisions."

"If I'd walked away, he never would have felt backed into a corner." He did this because I stayed on the team. I know it.

"None of that matters now. We're done. Look—I gotta go and tell the team what's happened."

We say our goodbyes, but I'm left standing in my kitchen with my weekend duffel bag, ready to catch a one-o'clock flight.

I can't believe Mitch would do this. I get how he didn't want me coming to Miami, but I don't get the why. It's a question I never stopped to ask. Yes, I know what Mitch said. It's dangerous. Women can't be bodyguards. But beneath all that chauvinism and the man-tantrums, what's the basis of his real objection?

My mind drifts back to the time we first met. It's the night of his housewarming party here in Houston. Georgie has left with Sam, and I'm standing in Mitch's bedroom, kissing him. I've only had a few beers—nowhere near tipsy—but I feel drunk from his touch and delicious scent—citrus, spices, man. Mitch's sex-lips move like a sensual poem over my neck and down my collarbone. His strong hands are like a love song, coaxing my body to melt for him. Everything about him is like a drug and gives me a rush.

I knew the moment I saw him in the flesh that he was the most beautiful guy I'd ever seen—way hotter than on all those sports magazine covers. The confident, warm look in his hazel eyes, the tall frame covered in lean muscle that filled out his clothes in a way that screamed pure masculinity, and the devilish smile on his lips. His presence filled a room like some god. More than anything, though, it was the way he made me feel when he looked at me. His house had been full of people, some of them gorgeous female models with the sorts of perfect bodies men can't resist. But I was the one he wanted to dance with. I was the one he wouldn't let go of as he mingled. We talked and laughed. We danced to ABBA and had the goofiest, best time. Most surprising was how easy it felt between us. New and exciting, but like we'd known each other for years. Whatever this thing was between us, it felt different than anything I'd ever experienced with a guy.

When he finally kissed me near the pool, under the stars, in front of dozens of people hanging around outside, I swore my heart almost stopped. For sure, my rational thinking did.

"Want to go upstairs?" His accent made his words sound a thousand times sexier. Of course, he could say anything—dirty socks, pond scum, hazardous waste—and make it sound hot.

"And leave your own party?" I asked.

He shrugged. "I hardly know any of these people. They're all friends of my agent or belong to the university." I already knew he had one semester left to finish his degree back in Australia, but he'd decided to start over here in the US. Now it makes sense, but at the time, I thought he might be a little on the wild and impulsive side. I mean, who quits school three months before graduation? Even if you're famous and rich, getting a degree is work. And he started college late due to his swimming schedule, then ended up taking a lighter load. So to quit after working five years for a degree, only to start over in another country? It made me wonder. Is he a flake? Is he just going to sleep with me and then lose my number? Or is he the type of guy who doesn't waste his time unless he's serious?

It's fifty-fifty. But if I didn't take a leap of faith, I'd never find out.

"Well." I pushed myself up on my tiptoes and planted a lingering kiss on Mitch's deliciously sexy lips. "If you really want to go upstairs..."

"I do." He took my hand and led me to his room, which was bigger than my entire house, with a private living room, kitchenette, enormous bathroom, and a trophy room. Before I knew it, his hands gripped my waist, and he was pulling me snugly against his hard frame. I could feel the part of him that he was so famous for straining against his black pants. The thought of him inside me, filling me, made me instantly wet and sinfully achy.

I reached for his blue oxford and began working the buttons.

"Wait." He grabbed my hand. "Would you mind if we just...got to know each other a little more?"

A guy who wants to talk? "Are you feeling all right? Is something wrong down there?" I glanced down at his enormous tent.

He chuckled. "No worries in that department. Just trying to turn over a new leaf is all."

"Wait. Are you, like...a secret nice guy?"

His light eyes lit up with amusement. "Don't tell anyone. I have a reputation to maintain."

I laughed, but then it hit me. Him not wanting to fuck me only made me want him more.

A pit formed in my stomach. I could seriously fall in love with this guy.

We spent the next hour talking as the party fizzled. He told me about his first trip to the Olympics and how he almost cried when he got up on that podium for his first gold medal.

“No. You? Cry?”

“I swear it.” He’d raised his hand in oath. “I held it in until I got to the locker room and then I wept like a baby.”

I could only imagine the joy of working so hard for so many years and then seeing your dream come true. What I liked most about him, though, was how he laughed at himself. I think only the most confident people can truly do that.

Then he went downstairs to make a quick, final appearance and let the staff know where he was in case they needed anything. Meanwhile, I tried to keep my head on straight. I couldn’t believe I was about to sleep with Mitch Hofer. Sex god. Closet gentleman. Smart. I didn’t know where this was heading, but I didn’t care. I’d never wanted someone this much.

He burst into the bedroom with a smile. “I think they’re all gone except for the people cleaning up. Want to go for a swim?”

“Hmmm…I didn’t bring a swimsuit.”

“No problem.” He took my hand and led me downstairs, through the bustling kitchen filled with servers packing up food.

Once outside at the Olympic-sized pool, Mitch released my hand, faced me, and took two steps back. The look in his caramel-colored eyes made my pulse spike and knees weak. Slowly, he unbuttoned his shirt, revealing his firm round pecs and wash-board stomach.

"Wow. Okay." I whooshed out a breath.

"Want to see more?"

I nodded like one of the dashboard dolls with the loosey-goosey bobble heads.

His grin grew wider, and then he stripped off his pants and underwear.

Oh… With the subtle turquoise glow of the pool lights, I could see every inch of his legendary cock hanging low between his muscular thighs.

My throat went dry. "Clearly your size has been exaggerated. We're going to have to give you a new nickname. How about baby carrot? You know like those cute little ones they serve at fancy restaurants?"

"Uh-huh. Sure." He laughed and crossed his arms over his chest, shamelessly flaunting what Mother Nature gave him. "Now it's your turn."

Oh boy. My body wasn't nearly as impressive. I had a narrow waist, decent-sized breasts, and a little extra meat on my hips and thighs. A normal woman.

"Turn around," I commanded.

"What?"

"Sorry, big boy, I'm not as brave as you. Don't have any gianormously impressive body parts that will blow your mind."

"I bet you're lovel—"

"You want to skinny-dip with those lights on in

the water? Then turn."

"Okay. Turning."

I quickly stripped and jumped into the pool so he couldn't peek. The water was warm, thank God. I hate being cold.

"Cheater." He jumped in after me. When his head emerged, our eyes locked, and like two giant magnets, our naked bodies slammed together. My breasts happily smashed against the swells of his smooth, hard pecs, and our tongues lapped in a voracious, hungry kiss. I flung my arms around his neck and wrapped my legs around his waist.

To my surprise, he unwound my legs, and when he lowered me, his long hard cock wedged tightly between the apex of my thighs. *Oh. Ohhh...*

I held back a moan. "I thought you said no sex," I panted.

He began rocking his hips, allowing his length to gently glide against my entrance and throbbing bud. "This is just very naughty foreplay."

"Oh. Good to know." Our lips found each other again, and he slowly brought my back to the wall of the pool. The cool tile felt refreshing on my shoulder blades given how the rest of my body sizzled, starting with the spot where the base of his shaft rubbed against my c-spot. Each soft pump of his hips made my bud ache more. More deliciously. More urgently.

I squeezed my thighs together, wanting more pressure. "Oh, God. I think I'm going to..." A euphoric explosion ignited, and I threw my head back with a moan. He ground his cock harder against me, sliding between the valley of my slick wet folds, but never penetrating me.

Oh God. Oh God. I felt his lips on mine but couldn't move, couldn't open my eyes. Not until one final orgasmic shudder thundered through me, releasing the last of the tension that had been building for hours.

So good. My nipples pearled into hard knots, and goose bumps erupted over every hypersensitive surface of my body.

Just as I began to regain consciousness, Mitch made one final thrust between my thighs. He groaned in my ear. It was a deep, animalistic, carnal sound that made my entire body spark right up again. I'd never heard anything so sexy.

Mitch's chest heaved with his heavy breaths, and he slumped against me, planting a lingering kiss on my lips.

"I'm going to have to drain my pool now." He cupped the back of my neck.

I chuckled, getting the jizz of the joke. "Ick. Okay. Now I'm imagining I have a colony of dying sperm coating my skin."

"I hear it's a great moisturizer. Want to take some home?" He chuckled.

"What? Ewww…" I laughed and swatted his shoulder, knowing he didn't mean it. *At least I hope?*

"Shower?" he offered.

Naked? Out of the pool? Could I do it? I wanted to. Really I did. But he was so perfect, so beautiful. I was just…me. Plain old Abi. On the other hand, I really liked this guy. I wanted this. I wanted him.

"Sure." I nodded. "Sounds good."

He left me in the pool and grabbed two fluffy towels from a cabinet in a nearby gazebo. When he returned, I climbed the small ladder and let him look. At everything. I figured that the darkness would help me warm up to the idea.

"You're gorgeous." He wrapped the towel around my shivering body and kissed me again. "I like you, Abi. A lot."

There was something in his tone—maybe the hint of vulnerability and tenderness—that threw me. I hadn't been expecting him to say those words and certainly not with such sincerity. "I like you, too?"

"You'd better." He kissed me again, and before I knew it, we were in his bed, the towels gone, our legs intertwined, and warm naked bodies pressed together. He wasn't hard, but I couldn't wait until the moment arrived because if a little dry humping—or wet humping since we had been in a pool?—felt this incredible, I couldn't imagine having real sex. The man was hung like a champion stallion, and he knew how to move his body. *Such coordination. Definitely a gold medalist.*

However, somewhere in between getting lost in the feel of his silky lips and hard body tightly fit against my soft curves, Mitch passed out. I tried to wake him, but finally gave up. Didn't help that he looked so happy and content.

"You're so handsome, Mitch." I traced the edges of his full lips and the ridges of his honey brown eyebrows, drinking him in.

How can this be possible? I'd seen this man dozens of times on TV or at the checkout stand, never realizing that he would be the guy I'd meet one night and have an amazing connection with.

I just might've been born to be with him. And not in some stalker, full back tattoo, gather his discarded belly-button fuzz to make a doll after I abduct him kind of way. He seemed equally drawn to me. *It's like everyone says; you just know when you meet the right person.*

I drifted off in his arms, and the next thing I knew, Mitch was shaking me the next morning. "Wake up. You have to go."

"Huh?" I cracked open my eyes to find a fully dressed Mitch scooping up my clothes and tossing them at my face.

"You heard me. Leave now."

I pulled the sheet over my bare breasts. "What happened? Is something wrong?" Because he looked angry—flat lips, eyebrows furrowed.

"No. I was drunk last night. It was fun, but I don't want to see you again."

Feeling confused and humiliated to be naked in front of him, I slid on my black cocktail dress. I grabbed my shoes, bra, and panties. Mitch must've brought them up from the pool.

"I'll show you out." He headed for the door, and I lapsed into my old habits—the shy awkward girl at a loss for words.

"But I...I..." My mouth flapped like two stale pancakes.

He dragged me by the hand, rushing me downstairs. When we got to the front door, he just stood there giving me a look, like he was disgusted for having touched me.

Was I that gross? Had his beer goggles tricked him into thinking I was one of his supermodel worshippers?

No, Abi. There's nothing wrong with you. Tell him to fuck off. Tell him he's an asshole. But when I opened my mouth, nothing came out.

He slammed the door in my face, and I cried right there on his doorstep. They were tears of frustration and shock more than anything else. How could I allow him to treat me like that? And what crawled up his muscled ass? His behavior was inhumane. It was cruel and unforgivable. Okay, maybe they were sad tears, too. I wanted our connection to be real. I thought it had been. *He played me.*

Now, knowing what I do, I suspect that Georgie was onto something. *Damn her! Always right!* There is definitely more to the story, but my anger wouldn't allow me to think compassionately or give

Mitch the benefit of the doubt. Don't know many women who would after what he did. My prince had turned into a frog. No. Wait. A frog turd.

But now I'm not so sure. Because clearly he'd rather fire his entire security detail and put his life at serious risk than place me in the crosshairs of whatever he thinks is about to go down.

I stand there in my kitchen, duffel bag in hand, with one mental foot already out the door. Part of me knows I shouldn't get on that plane. It would be stupid to try to protect Mitch all by myself. I have almost no experience. On the other hand, what if my gut is right? What if Mitch isn't the bad guy he portrays?

You idiot. Of course he's not. A real asshole wouldn't fire his bodyguards just to keep them safe.

But a closet-nice-guy would.

I rush out the door to catch my plane.

CHAPTER FOURTEEN

MITCH

I don't believe in fear. Not like a normal person. And I give most of the credit to years of hard training focusing the mind on one thing and one thing only: winning. Fear can be a good motivator, too, but it erodes self-confidence and drains away precious energy.

Yeah, and right now you could use more of it. The truth is I have too much male pride. It's why I refuse to let those Kemmler bastards win.

I swim six hours a day, six days a week. I propel myself the equivalent of two hundred and eighty thousand meters a month, which is about one hundred seventy-six miles. This doesn't include time with weights or my psychology coach, who helps rid my mind of doubt. I've had very little social life while attending university, going to competitions, and preparing myself for gold. It's my pride that's kept me going day in and day out, when I just want to drink a pint, eat a pizza, and head to the beach. Pride fuels me when I don't think I can make one more lap. It tells me that looking like an arse and coming in last is not an option.

Neither is this gut I'm starting to grow again. Must lay off the Italian subs.

I rub the soft spot just below my six-pack. *No worries. You're still a handsome devil,* says my pride. And now it's telling me I'm right to be here in Miami, unguarded when there's a price on my head.

Debating ordering room service before meeting up with my mate Ash at the bar down the way, I sit up from the king-size bed, where I've been sulking for the better part of the afternoon. I don't know if I'm doing the right thing here. "Of course you are. You're winning."

And winning means swimming. I make a quick call to the concierge to let them know I'm coming, before I grab my towel and head down to the pool.

ABI

The two-and-a-half-hour flight from Houston to Miami felt like ten hours. In hell. My mind kept repeating images of Mitch being gunned down on the catwalk. Making my fear worse, his bathing suit was some hideous Chucky doll face.

So scary. But that's my mind for ya. When my emotions run high, my brain does all sorts of weird stuff, like overreact or instantly leap to the worst possible scenario. Then it starts trying to imagine how that feels and what I'd do. I call it nightmare mode. Of course, ninety-nine-point-nine-nine-nine percent of the time, everything turns out fine.

Just like now. Nothing to worry about. I'm sure Mitch is okay.

Almost to the hotel, I realize I forgot to turn my phone back on. I press the power-up button and wince. "Oh...mistake." There are ten messages from Sam, three from Georgie, and one from my mom, all of them wondering where I am. "*Please tell me this is a joke, Abigail,*" says my mother, who sounds beyond pissed because she's used my full name. "*Please tell me you did not get a job with Sam like Georgie said! Call me immediately, young lady.*"

I can't believe my best friend ratted me out. Of course, I never told her not to say anything.

"Too late now," I mumble to myself. Besides, this is my last job. I'll either die or convince Mitch to run with me, but my bodyguard days are over. This is way too crazy.

My cab pulls up to the beachfront hotel where Mitch is staying, and I sprint to the registration counter. "Hi. Um...I'm supposed to be meeting..." *Shit, shit, shit! What's Mitch's cover name?* It was on the sheet Sam gave the team, but I left it at home. "Ummm...Nemo...Thorpe?" I think that's right. Nemo is that little fish, and Ian Thorpe is another famous Australian swimmer and Mitch's biggest inspiration. I know this because he mentioned it in an interview. Not that I'm obsessed with Mitch like the rest of the world, but the news played a lot of clips during the last Olympics. It was hard to ignore. So when Sam gave us Mitch's code name, it stuck in my mind because it was possibly the worst code name ever for a swimmer who's trying to be discreet.

"Sorry, miss," says the young woman behind the counter, "but there's no Nemo Thorpe staying here."

Dammit. "Um, well, is there anyone with that last name? A Dori? How about a Jamie or a Frazer? Maybe Loki or Thor or something?"

"Uh, no. Sorry. Perhaps you should call your friend and confirm where he's staying."

I know he's here at this hotel. I memorized the floor plan. There are six exits on each floor, excluding the elevators. Each hallway is laid out in a cross formation to accommodate the rectangular shape of the building. There are fifteen floors, the upper ones have suites, but the penthouse takes up the entire top floor.

"Miss?" the woman says, eyeing the customers behind me.

Urgh…! "I will absolutely kill him—metaphorically speaking, of course—but did my jerk of a boyfriend check in under his real name?" I lean in to whisper, "Mitch Hofer."

The woman raises a brow. Her lack of denial confirms it.

"Wow. Really? He used his actual name. Can

you give me a key to that floor?" It's secure and no one gets up to the penthouse without an access card.

"My apologies. But giving out room keys to nonguests is against policy."

Well, good for her, sticking to safety protocols.

"But," she adds, "the house phone is over on that table if you want to reach any of our rooms."

"Thank you." I rush over and ask the hotel operator for Mitch. I still don't know exactly what I'm going to say, but I imagine it's going to sound something like... *You're such an epic ass! And I'm not buying this alpha-male pig crap anymore!*

After ten rings, I start to panic. He's not answering the phone. I'm about to rush back to the reception and tell them to call hotel security when I catch a glimpse of Mitch strolling across the far end of the lobby.

"Oh, thank God!" He's okay. *See! I always overreact.*

I rush after him, noting that he's wearing a pair of blue board shorts and a white T-shirt. *He's going for an evening swim.* The towel around his neck is a dead giveaway.

When I get to the iron gates surrounding the pool, I see a big ol' "Closed for Maintenance" sign.

Spoiled brat. They closed the pool for him.

He's about to jump in when I notice something completely out of place. "What the fuck?" A white power cord is plugged into the outlet of the nearby pool-caddy hut and dangling in the water.

Oh no! "Mitch! Mitch! Don't get in the pool!"

But as loud as I'm yelling, he doesn't hear me. He must be wearing earplugs or something.

Shit. Shit! I look around me and spot a trash can a few feet away. It's the type with a cement base and heavy steel lid with a little swinging door. I hop on top of it and jump the fence. The landing nearly breaks my ankle.

Ow… I get to my feet. *Super ow!* "Mitch!" I yell and hop on one foot, praying he'll hear me.

He doesn't.

Time seems to slow as I watch him go to the edge of the pool, his body leaning forward to propel into the water.

"Mitch! Stop!" I dive for him, grabbing the back of his shorts just as he's about to lean into his jump.

"What the!" He tries to get upright, but the next thing I know he's twisting his body and falling back toward the water, his arms windmilling.

It's a split-second decision, but I don't know what else to do. I slide my legs forward, dig the heels of my tennis shoes into the cement, and release his shorts. I reach for his hand, grab on, and yank back with all my weight, like a rower fighting for the finish line. Mitch propels forward and lands on top of me with a grunt.

"Abi! What the bloody hell, woman?" he barks.

"Get. Off. Can't. Breathe." I push, and he rolls to my side.

"What are you doing here?" He sounds pissed.

"Wind. Knocked," I sputter, gulping for air.

"Okay. Okay. Just relax. It'll pass." He presses his warm hand to my cheek. "Just relax."

Finally, my lungs kick in, and I gasp. "Oh, Jesus." I lay there panting for several moments, thanking my lucky Aussie stars that we didn't both go in.

"What the devil are you doing, you crazy sheila?"

I point to the water. "Cord. Electrocution."

He looks at the pool and then me. Pool. Then me. "What the hell?"

"Yeah." I nod frantically. "Exactly."

"How'd you know?"

"I just got here and noticed it."

"You…saved me," he says with disbelief. "Again."

Damned straight.

His body partially covering mine, he stares into my eyes. I can't read his thoughts, but I know, with everything in my heart, that I'm seeing the real Mitch again. The same guy I met that night back in Houston.

He affectionately strokes my hair. "And you just happened to be here? At the right time?"

I nod.

"Abi, I'm…I'm so sorry about all this."

I move to sit up, and he kneels in front of me.

"Mitch, why did you come alone? Why would you be so stupid?"

He glances at the ground between us. "I'm asking myself the same question."

"We have to get out of here. Now. Whoever did this is posing as an employee of the hotel. How else would they know you were about to go for a swim?"

The vacant look in his eyes tells me he's not listening to a word I'm saying.

"Mitch. Mitch!" I grab his shoulder and give it a firm shake.

"We could be dead right now. Both of us," he mumbles, like it's some big epiphany.

Who knows? Maybe that cord would have shocked the hell out of us and then tripped the breaker. Maybe it would have sizzled us unconscious. I'm just happy we didn't have to find out.

"We have to go now." I glance up at the hundreds of windows overlooking the pool. Whoever did this is watching. I know it. But Mitch is still in some other place. "Mitch! We have to go!"

His eyes focus on mine like he's just seen a ghost. Or the Grim Reaper? "There's nowhere to hide, Abi. Wherever I go, they'll find me."

"You don't know that." I give his brawny shoulders another shake.

"I do. The Kemmlers have friends in high places."

"So what are you saying? Because, screw me, it sounds like you're throwing in the towel."

"I'm saying that…I don't know."

The man actually looks disoriented, like he's in

shock.

"Let's go back to your room," I say in the calmest voice possible. "You'll grab your things, and we'll get the hell out of here." I don't know where we'll go, but maybe that's a good thing. If I don't know, then no one else does either.

"Right."

We stand, and I jerk that cord from the socket so no one else gets hurt. "Come on. Hurry."

We walk briskly toward the lobby and wait for an empty elevator. I don't know who is who at this point.

Bingo! We get one, but I pray the entire way up that no one will board.

"Fuck." I squeeze Mitch's hand as the elevator stops a few floors shy of the penthouse. I reach for my gun, fearing it might be the disgruntled assassin who witnessed his failed murder attempt just now. "Double fuck." I didn't bring a gun. Sam planned to arm us when we arrived, so I left my peashooter in my sock drawer.

"Punch whoever walks through that door," I say.

"Huh?"

"Punch 'em. As hard as you can."

"What if it's not the person who's trying to kill me?" he asks.

"We won't know until it's too late. And a lawsuit is better than death."

"Right."

The doors slide open, and in steps a young woman wearing all pink. She's holding a baby dressed in matching colors. Mitch pulls back his fist. The woman screams and runs away.

"Sorry! Thought you were someone else!" Mitch yells. "I'd never punch a baby!"

"She, on the other hand," I mumble, "she looked way too girly. Definitely suspicious." I poke the button to close the doors. "Hurry, you piece of shit!"

"Abi, Abi, slow down. What are we doing?" Mitch seems to be back, his brain firing on all cylinders.

"We're getting the hell out of Dodge." I repeatedly jab at the *close door* button, because everyone knows that pressing harder makes the elevator magically move faster.

"No. I mean…what are *we* doing?"

I blink and stare into those hypnotic eyes. "What do you mean?"

"You can't be here. You can't protect me," he says with a sadness so deep it instantly weighs me down.

"But I can, Mitch," I say softly. "I already have."

His eyes flicker with emotion. "Yes. But what if you're not so lucky next time?" He reaches out and runs a rough thumb over my bottom lip. "This is my battle. Not yours."

His concern for me only makes me more determined to save him. "Mitch, we're leaving. And if you're the man I think you are, the good man my gut tells me you are, then you'll realize this is a team event, not an individual heat or a battle of the sexes. So when these doors open, you will move that tight ass, because by my estimates, whoever electrified that pool knows the job wasn't done, and we only have a few minutes before they figure out how to get into the penthouse." I press my hand to his stubbled cheek. "I know you're strong. I know you're determined and proud. But for once in your life, listen to a woman who has a knack for protecting the people she loves."

The elevator doors slide open to the penthouse floor, and his lips part with hesitation.

"What?" I bark.

"Woman, be my bodyguard. Because I wouldn't trust anyone else to protect all this awesomeness."

I smile, and it comes from deep inside. "Smartass. Come on." I take his hand, and we charge into his suite. It's truly impressive with a partial view of the ocean and hotel strip. If we weren't about to die, I'd be snapping off selfies.

"Hurry," I say. "You need shoes, pants, and any cash you've got."

"Just carrying a few hundred."

"Then we'll have to stop and get more on the way to…to…I don't know where we're going, but I'll call Sam." He'll know where we can hide and how to get there without leaving a paper trail.

"Abi?" Mitch looks at me as he gathers his stuff,

shoving it into a small carry-on.

"Yeah?"

"Thank you."

"Don't mention it. It's always been my dream to save a world-famous swimmer from drowning in his own stupidity."

"No. I really mean it. Thank you for everything. As insane as it sounds for a guy like me to say, I don't see myself surviving this without you."

My heart swells with emotion. I hate that this is happening to him—to us—but part of me is crazy happy. He's alive. I'm alive. We're going to get through this together. "Can you promise to say that again when we're safe? Otherwise, I might not remember it and I kinda want to."

"I'm not done. If we don't make it, you should know how sorry I am for the way I treated you. I thought if you were near me, it would make me weak. You'd get hurt." He looks down at the black shirt wadded in his hands. "I feel responsible for the people in my life. I can't help it."

Oh. No. You did *not* just say that. "Stop it! Stop being so perfect, or I swear…" I shake my head to gather my emotions. "I swear I'll fall in love with you, and then where would that leave you, huh? You'd have a bodyguard who leaves drool puddles everywhere. So embarrassing."

A hint of a smile cracks his lips, but he says nothing.

"Let's go." We head toward the door. I look

through the peephole to confirm the small lobby, leading to the elevator and stairwell, is vacant. "We take the stairs, get a few blocks away, and then grab a taxi. We'll stop in an hour to call Sam from a payphone if those even exist anymore. I'm not really sure, but we'll just have to figure that out. Ready?"

Because my heart sure isn't. I feel like I'm going to have one of those awesome panic attacks again and pass out.

"Abi?"

"Yes?"

"Just one last thing." Mitch grabs me and presses his soft lips to mine. My heart goes from panicked to a serious pitter. Or patter? Who cares. I only know that kissing him feels like the best drug in the world. It's sensual and delicious, but more than anything, it feels so right. Kissing him fills a hole in my heart I didn't know I had.

He pulls away and rubs the tip of his nose against mine. "I'm ready."

Good. Because if I'm right, it's going to take a miracle for us to get out alive. He jerks open the door, and we both freeze. A large blond man is standing there with a gun in his hand.

"*'Ello*, mate." The man grins sadistically.

"Ash?" Mitch frowns. "Please tell me you're not part of this."

"A million cryptos, brother. For a friend who left me the minute he got famous. In my opinion, I'm being overpaid, but I'll take the money anyway."

"Ash, I didn't leave you." Mitch's voice is low and calm, but he sounds devastated. "You had a drug problem and wouldn't deal with it no matter how hard I tried to convince you. I was happier than fuck when you called and said you'd dealt with it."

I watch the two men having this debate, but it's clear Ash is mental. His hand is shaking. His face is pale and sweaty. Call it women's intuition, but I know he's about to shoot that gun.

Okay. Okay. What did the instructor teach me in bootcamp? Think. Think! There was that whole kung fu slap-the-barrel trick, but I wasn't very good at it. Then there was the lunge, lift, and thrust technique, where you grab the gun with both hands and lift so the barrel points upward. Then you go in close and give the old nuts a little hug with your kneecap.

No, Ash is too far away. There are four feet between us. The only other thing I can think of is—

A sinister twitch in Ash's eyes triggers me to jump in front of Mitch just as a loud noise cracks through the air. Something slams into my chest, sending me flying back. At the same time, Mitch lunges forward and hammers Ash's face, knocking him out.

I lie there, completely confused, while Mitch grabs the gun and rushes to my side.

"Abi!" Mitch's eyes fill with terror. "Just hold still. Don't move, okay? I'm calling for help."

I can't breathe. The pressure in my chest is mixed with the worst kind of pain imaginable.

"Mitch," I croak. "Mitch?"

"I'm here! I'm here. Just stay calm, okay. They're coming."

"Mitch, this is all your fault. You're such a stubborn assbag."

He gives me a strange look, like he's unsure if I'm joking. Which I am. In any case, he doesn't seem to appreciate my humor.

I decide to double down. "If I die, I'm going to haunt you for the rest of your life."

CHAPTER FIFTEEN

MITCH

"Any news on Abi Carter? Is she going to be all right?" I ask the nurse who whizzes past me in the ER, intent on ignoring me or anyone else who gets in her way. But after one hour of zero news, I'm at the end of my rope.

I follow her down the brightly lit hallway, ready to use whatever charms I've got. "'Scuze me, miss." I tap her shoulder, and she stops.

"Oh. It's you again. Like I said, you're not immediate family. I can't tell you anything."

"How about two free tickets to the 2020 Olympics in Tokyo? All expenses paid, eh?" I ramp up the accent, hoping it will buy me some points. American sheilas love the accent.

Her face lights up. "Ohmygod! You're that swimmer guy."

I smile proudly and straighten my spine. "Yes. I'm Mitch Hofer."

Her expression turns stone cold. "The answer is still no." She turns to leave, but I grab her hand. I will do whatever it takes to find out what's happening with Abi. I owe that woman my life. I owe her everything.

"Right. Well, you either tell me how she is, or I'll go right outside to that mob of reporters and tell them how heartless you are. My sweet, loving...fiancée might be dead and you won't give me the time of day. The press will hound you the rest of your life," I glance at her name badge, "Ruth K."

"Fine." She crosses her arms. "Go ahead. You think you scare me?"

Damned woman! "Is there anything I can do to make you change your mind? Anything at all?" I reach out and make a little circle with the pad of my thumb on her arm.

A coy smile crawls across her lips, and her eyes slowly move downtown. "On second thought, I think we can work something out."

ABI

I'm lying on the gurney in the ER, feeling like the luckiest girl in the world from all of the painkillers they've pumped into me, when Mitch enters the small curtained cubicle. His face is all hard lines and frownies. "Mitchipoo! Where you been, baby?"

He grunts something unintelligible.

"Uh-oh, is my little polliwog cranky? Did someone forget to feed you a fly?" I crack up.

"What the hell did they give you?" He sounds displeased.

What a buzzkill. "Hey! I'm having fun here, so shoo, baby frog. Shoo! Because I'm a big hungry owl," I stretch out my powerful talons, "and I'm going to eat you legs first so I can see the expression on your face."

"I just had to show some nurse my cock so I could hear that you're perfectly fine. Then I had to let her touch it so I could get in here and yell at you. Why the bloody fuck did you jump in front of that bullet? You could have gotten yourself killed!"

"I dunno."

"And why didn't you tell me you were wearing a vest, eh?"

"Oops! No blood." I don't know why, but I can't stop laughing. Mitch, on the other hand, only seems to be getting angrier.

"I was worried, Abi. Genuinely worried. They took you in the ambo, and I thought for sure you'd kicked the bucket."

"I only kick swimmers. Come closer."

He shakes his head, those incredible sex-lips tightening into an angry little snarl. "Stop acting childish and listen to me."

I suddenly don't feel like laughing anymore. *God. He's being so mean. I'm in here because of him and… Why isn't he kissing me? He should be kissing me and telling me he loves me. But he's not. And now… What was I thinking? Oh. That I'm mad at him.* "Nope. I'm not going to listen to you. And you and your big old bearded clam hammer, zipper burrito, meat rocket, cocktopus, one-eyed crotch dragon can just…suck it." *Damn. These drugs make me so creative!*

"Such a vulgar little thing." He folds his thick arms over his broad chest. "And just when I was starting to like you."

"Really? You were? Because I liked you, Mitchipoo. I really did. And then you turned out to be a slack-jawed knuckle-dragger."

"Wow. That hurts."

"Not as bad as this." I yank on the neck of my gown to give him a lookie-see of the giant red mark on my chest that's turning purple. "It's like a mood ring. On my tit. And right now, my tit is sad, Mitch. So sad."

"Stop that." He pulls up my gown and covers what appears to be my entire boob hanging out. "Bloody hell. When will the meds wear off?"

"Hopefully never, because this is the first time in months that I've felt…weeee! Happy! I don't even care about my mom and me losing our house or the fact she's going to be closing her business because some prick made her decorate his house in a Rambo theme and then wanted his money back. I don't even care that I can't afford my final semester of college and that the job Sam gave me would have made it all…better." I toss my hands in the air. "Don't care! See!" I giggle.

Mitch shakes his head remorsefully, though I'm unsure why. "You should've told me. I would have helped you."

"You? Help *me*? You kicked my ass to the curb like a…an old armchair all covered in crusty boogers and cigarette burns."

"So descriptive." He grimaces. "Well, I said I was sorry, Abi. You know I had my reasons. Your life being one of them. I found out that someone had been caught with a knife hiding in a closet the morning after the party. The security team let him get away before the police showed up, which is why I ended up hiring Sam. But it was a red flag. I couldn't risk you getting hurt."

"Really? Awww… You're so sweet." I mean it. He smells like a Tootsie Roll. I wiggle my nose, wondering if I'm imagining it.

"No. I'm not sweet, but I am going to make things right. Like I should've from the get-go."

"Okeydokey. I'm just going to take a nap now. Could you call my mom? Tell her I'm on drugs and realllly happy, okay?" My eyes feel like two lead weights are pulling them closed. "Phone is over there. My password is 'I hate Mitch.'"

"Of course it is."

When I wake several hours later, I find I've been moved from the ER into another room. The TV is on and Georgie is sitting by my bedside.

"Hey, what are you doing here?" I mumble, scrubbing my face with my hands. My head feels like I've been doing Benadryl shots. So fuzzy.

"Oh, you're awake!" She springs from the chair and hugs me. "Your mom's plane just landed. She's on her way, okay?"

"Owww..." I groan from the pressure of the embrace.

"Oh. Sorry. I'm just so happy you're okay." She releases me and slaps the top of my head.

"Hey." I rub the spot.

"Do you know how lucky you are, Abi? What were you thinking coming to Miami alone?"

"Why does everyone keep yelling? Mitch is alive because of me."

"I can't speak for whoever this 'everyone' is, but as far as I go, it's because I love you. Mitch, not so much."

"He's not as bad as we thought, Georgie."

She grumbles something that sounds like "Dirtybastardclownfucker," but I can't be sure.

"Where's Mitch now?" I mumble.

"He skedaddled the minute I showed up. Something to do with an interview or his Weeno party." She pauses. "Damn, I hate that name. Sounds like I'm two years old, trying to say 'wiener party.'"

I'd smile, but I'm too disappointed. I somehow believed that things between Mitch and I had changed, but if that were true, he'd be here right now.

Why do I always get my hopes up like this? It's ridiculous, frankly.

"Hey. No long faces," Georgie says. "You get to go home. You're alive. In fact, the doctor said your X-rays were all clear—no cracked ribs or anything—so it's just lots of rest and fancy painkillers for you."

I'm about to remind her how much I hate taking pills when something, or should I say *someone*, catches my eye. "Ohmygod. That's Mitch on the TV. Turn it up."

"Huh?" Georgie glances at the screen. "What the hell is he doing?" She grabs the remote on the little side table, which I hadn't seen.

With dozens of microphones shoved in his face, Mitch is discussing his uncle's death. "…his murder is public knowledge; however, the details surrounding the motives are not."

"Why?" one reporter yells out. "Why are you coming forward now?"

"The authorities asked me to keep the details quiet given the ongoing investigation, but the truth is I didn't want any of this going public either. After my uncle Albert was shot, I only thought about myself. How much I missed him, how angry I felt, and how I would do everything in my power not to let the assh—*bleep!*—destroy my career." Mitch draws a solemn breath. "But to answer the question, I'm finally coming forward because there's a woman inside this hospital who took a bullet for me, all because I didn't want to place myself in the middle of a scandal that would detract from my professional career. But it's time to get the full story out there. I don't care if this starts a PR war with these people or opens me up to defamation lawsuits due to the lack of solid proof."

Mitch goes on to tell the press about the WWII photos implicating Ralf Kemmler of war crimes and how the man in jail for murdering his uncle is really a hit man. "The Kemmlers hired Kristoff Bones because they didn't want their family's past to hurt their profits, something I'm sure they'll deny doing. But what they can't lie about are the photos."

"Are you one hundred percent sure you saw Ralf Kemmler in the photos?" a female reporter yells out.

Mitch nods. "Yes, he is the man in the pictures, but I think it would be easier if everyone took a look for themselves. I kept digital copies of the photos and just now posted them on my Instagram and Twitter accounts."

The press starts buzzing, but Mitch ignores them and looks right at the camera. "I'm sorry, Abi, for what I said about chicks. You are the best bodyguard a big, strong, totally-secure-with-himself guy could ever ask for. But more importantly, you are an amazing woman. I'm lucky to have met you." He winks.

I tear up. In my eyes, he's validated what my heart was trying to tell me all along. Mitch was worth saving. I only wish he'd come out with all this sooner. It makes it really difficult for the Kemmlers to kill him since the world would know they're behind it. I also wish he'd said all of that nice stuff about me to my face. It's what I'd do if someone saved my life.

"Wow. That really was sweet." Georgie quickly grabs her phone, making lots of taps. "Ohmygod. Look!" She shows me the screen. There's an old black-and-white photo of a bunch of sad, wet, grimy-looking Nazi soldiers standing in formation and saluting some super-duper short guy with an eye patch and the world's biggest handlebar mustache.

"Yikes. That's Ralf Kemmler? I can't believe he murdered a bunch of people and then moved on to write Valentine's cards." The worst part is that the vintage ones are everyone's favorite Kemmler cards. "Now every time I see one that says *You're sweet enough to eat*, I'm going to get the willies." I shudder.

"Yeah. Kind of puts a damper on their black-and-white Cutie Kittens cards, too. Makes you wonder what happened to them after the photoshoot."

We both sit in silence for a moment, pondering the ick factor of the situation.

"Abi! Abi!" My mother bursts into the room, her face stained with tears and her ponytail lopsided.

"I'm okay, Mom."

She bends down to give me a quick hug and

then gets to the finger shaking. "I don't care if you're twenty-one. You are so grounded, little girl. What were you thinking playing bodyguard? Huh?" She swats the top of my head.

"Ouch. What's with you guys?" I gripe.

"I'll wait outside and let you two catch up." Georgie leaves the room despite my protests. I've come a long way in the "speaking my mind" department, but my mother is the exception. I've never quite been able to tell her what I'm thinking or how I'm feeling. Not so much because I'm afraid of her as I am afraid for her. She is so sensitive.

"I'm sorry, Mom. I just didn't want to worry you. Not when you've got so much else on your plate."

She takes the chair next to me and grabs my hand. "Honey, but those are my problems to fix. Not yours. Yes, I might lose my business because of my ex-client, but I know how to start over."

"But what about our house?"

She shrugs. "I can't lie. I'll miss it. But at the end of the day, it's just a house, a thing. It doesn't define me."

"I know that, but it's where you lived with Dad. Where we had birthdays and Christmases and—"

"And those are all right here." She places her hand over her heart. "They're not going anywhere. And who's to say a fresh start wouldn't be good for me, my career, and my home?"

A fresh start. "But you love interior design."

"I did. I do. But life is short, and I wouldn't mind starting a different business. I like a challenge. And I've already decided I want to downsize, so that's that. I've found a realtor, and he assures me the house will sell quickly. I can use the money to find something else I love to do. Plus, you'll get to finish your bachelor's."

"Oh, Mom..." She already took a second mortgage and maxed out her credit to keep us afloat. Now she'll lose her home? "There has to be another way."

"Abi," she squeezes my arm, "you've always been so fiercely protective of the people you love. Even when you were little, you'd rather invent these crazy stories about how your shirt got torn or how your dinner ended up on the floor."

It's true. When I was in the first grade, some boy in my class decided to take a pair of scissors and cut a hole in the back of my shirt. I told my mom and dad that I tore it on the jungle gym. Of course, the teacher ended up telling her the truth. On more than one occasion, I also "accidentally" spilled my food on the floor because it tasted horrible. Really, I just didn't want to hurt my mom's feelings. Her cooking isn't always so great, though she does make a mean lasagna. Still, my mom eventually figured it out after I made too many messes.

My mom goes on, "Now that you're all grown up, you're trying to be this one-woman army, Abi. But you know what? Shutting me out, pushing people away, and lying doesn't protect anyone. It just hurts the people who love you."

Man. Now I feel like a complete ass. Part of it's because I'm realizing how much I've hurt my mom, but the other part has to do with Mitch. He lied to me. He pushed me away. All because he wanted to protect me. If I'd just stopped for one lousy second and asked myself what was really going on, I might have seen the truth.

Suddenly, I feel like a knuckle-dragging she-moron because I should know better. Instead, I spent all these months stewing over how he treated me. I hated him, I had fantasies about casting a spell that would give him a perma-limpy, and I allowed my anger to blind me.

The irony is that I think his protective side is sexy. He's literally willing to do anything for the people he cares about. *Even making a statement to the press that puts him smack in the middle of a huge scandal.* From this day forward, Mitch Hofer will be known as the Olympic swimmer who brought down a global company. I'm guessing that's not why he worked so hard to win four gold medals. I'm also guessing that the sponsors would rather pay a celebrity who will make their products the center of attention versus a WWII war criminal and his company.

"I'm so sorry, Mom. I should have told you about the job and why I took it."

"All is forgiven. Just as long as you promise to

never. Ever. Evereverever! Do this again. I can't believe you took a job as a bodyguard."

"I'm actually kind of good at it." I look at my mother and her bloodshot eyes. "Not that I want to do this forever. I mean, I know I won't. Not full-time anyway. I have to finish school, but for the time being, I enjoy it and I could really use the money."

She sighs. "I…I…then I support you. But you've got to promise you'll be careful and not keep any more secrets."

This is a huge step for her, and while I know she'll still worry, a heavy burden has been lifted. Protecting her, lying to her, worrying about her had taken on a life of its own. It created distance between us. But if she can handle my new job, then she can handle anything.

"Yay! I love when everyone's happy!" Georgie pops back in the room. I suspect she was listening the entire time.

"Yes, and I promise no more secrets." Lying to my mom isn't who I am.

"By the way, Sam just called. Said Mitch is with him, safe and sound." Georgie looks uncomfortable all of a sudden.

I frown, waiting for more info, but Georgie doesn't volunteer it. "So? Where are they?"

"At the Weeno fashion show," Georgie says reluctantly.

I sigh with grief. "So he really went."

"Sam said it's part of Mitch's contract. He didn't want to get sued for breach. The good news is that the Kemmlers are outed. Sam doubts they'll go after Mitch when every eye in the world is watching them."

"Isn't Mitch still a key witness in his uncle's murder?" I ask.

"Yes, which is why Sam went to make sure security is tight enough."

I get that Mitch's statement to the press has put a spotlight on this Kristoff guy and the Kemmlers, but I don't like letting Mitch just roam free. What if they're not done with him?

"Don't look so worried," says Georgie. "Sam will keep an eye on things, and Mitch is skipping the after-party. He said he'll come straight back here when he's done," Georgie adds.

"Well, I'm going to the hotel, so…"

"Baby, why don't you stay here and rest?" my mom suggests.

"I'm okay. Even the doctors said so, and right now a long hot bath sounds wonderful." I need to decompress and digest. None of this is sitting right with me because I have to wonder if Mitch really meant everything he said to the cameras. And if so, why didn't he say it to my face? It leaves me questioning him again, which drives me crazy. My heart wants to trust him. It wants to believe there's something special between us. But my brain tells me I've been down this road before and, more importantly, actions speak louder than words.

CHAPTER SIXTEEN

My mom decided to catch a flight back home to Houston so she can meet with her lawyer first thing in the morning and then start getting the house ready for viewing in two weeks. As for Georgie, she stayed with me to get things settled with the hospital and take me back to the hotel. Oddly enough, I feel all right. The mark on my chest smarts, but the rest of my body is in fair shape after that drug-induced power nap. My mind is a different story.

"Stop it," Georgie scolds from the back of the Uber. "Mitch is going to be fine."

I remove my slightly nibbled index finger from my mouth. "Is it that obvious?"

"I don't blame you for worrying. I mean, there've been two attempts on his life in the space of a week."

"Three. Someone tried to electrocute him in the pool."

Georgie's face contorts. "Seriously?"

I bob my head. "I think it was his friend, that

Ash guy. By the way, what happened to him?" With all the commotion, I forgot to ask.

"The police hauled him off."

"And how was Mitch when you saw him? Was he upset?"

Georgie toggles her lips from side to side. "I couldn't tell. He was kind of acting normal, like he did in that press conference."

So his good friend tries to kill him, shoots me, and he seemed okay with it all? "I really need to get to know him better, because if you tried to barbeque me for money, I'd be devastated."

Georgie reaches into her purse and grabs a piece of mint gum. "Want some?"

"No, thanks."

She pops a stick in her mouth and starts talking and chewing. "Well, it's pretty clear that Mitch is handling things the way most men do; he's shoving it all down a deep dark hole and pretending it never happened. Plus, Mitch is super competitive, and I'm guessing he sees sulking as something only losers do. Henry is the exact same way."

Her brother Henry is a pro-football player and a big, giant muscly teddy bear. On the inside anyway. On the outside he is driven, fierce, and extremely competitive.

"What is it about jocks being such feeling-haters?" she adds. "I swear I could never date an athlete. Except for Mitch. Actually pretty much all swimmers. They make me wet." She cracks up. "Get it? They're always in water and..."

I glare at Georgie.

"Sorry. Too soon for humor?"

"Yes. Especially because..."

"You want to go to the show, don't you?" she asks accusatorily.

I bite my lower lip and nod. I need to see Mitch and confront him. I don't know where we stand, and if what I feel for him isn't mutual, then I'd rather know right now. "Maybe just to make sure everything's safe?"

"You're so protective. All right. We can go, but just for a few minutes. You need rest, girl, and I promised your mom to keep an eye on you." Georgie tells the driver that we're changing course.

"Thanks, G-cow. You're the beast," I say and give her hand a squeeze.

"No problem, Flabi. I'd moo anything for you."

"Damn. Now, *this* was a mistake." It's early evening in front of a convention center near downtown Miami, and I'm watching people filing into the Weeno show while Georgie argues with Sam on her cell phone to get us inside. I'd talk to him myself, but I'm too busy letting my mouth hang open. I've never seen so many outrageous swimsuits. I'm talking about the guests. It's like one giant costume party.

"Hey," I elbow Georgie, "that guy is dressed as a duck pond." He has on a blue bodysuit with plastic lily pads and rubber duckies glued to it.

"Shhh. I'm trying to listen." She turns her back while I'm sure I look like a cat who's just discovered the joy of ping-pong spectatorship. One by one, tree frogs, bananas, and people wearing nothing but innertubes stroll by.

"Is it Halloween? I don't get it," I mutter to no one.

A woman in a green mermaid outfit stops next to me. "Darn it. Where's that damned ticket?" She digs through her clamshell purse.

"Excuse me." I tap her glitter-covered shoulder. "What's with all the costumes?"

She stops her search to give me a look. "You've never been to the Weeno show?"

Oh...well, excuuuse me. "Can't say I've had the pleasure."

"Uh. Okay. Well, it's a thing."

I never knew mermaids were so judgy. "And what, pray tell, is the meaning of this *thing*, oh single-flippered one?"

She looks at me like I just fell off the lame-o-nerd truck, which is absolutely correct. Got the dents to prove it.

"Well, you know they, like, have these parties after the runway show and give away prizes for the best costumes. They even pick one person's design to be featured in next year's collection." She leans in a little and speaks from the side of her mouth. "But rumor has it, they won't be around next year. No one's buying their stuff."

Not really a surprise. Their "stuff" is hideous, not to mention, any guy who wears a Weeno, Mitch excluded, is immediately pegged as an inchworm.

"That's unfortunate," I say.

"Yeah, well, the only reason people came this year is to see Mitch Hofer. In the flesh." She winks. "Oh. And the free drinks are good, too. Ha! Found it!" She produces a ticket from her purse. "See ya inside."

"Sure thing." I give her a polite little wave. *So this will be the company's last show, then.*

"All right." Georgie stashes her phone in her jeans pocket. "Sam will be out in a minute with our passes. But be forewarned. He is super annoyed I'm here."

"Annoyed or angry?" I ask.

"Mmmm…not sure. Why?"

Because Sam isn't always so forthcoming with the facts. If he's angry, then maybe he's more concerned about safety than he's letting on.

"No reason," I reply.

"Wow! Did you see that guy? He's dressed as a fisherman. Wait, why is his fish coming out of his pants?" Georgie squints, her eyes zeroing in on his crotch.

"That's not a fish. It's his dick covered in sequins."

"Not that I'm a glamour queen, but this is some of the worst fashion ever." Georgie is more of a casual girl. Her jeans and gray sweatshirt outfit, like the one she has on now, is pretty much her go-to. I've still got on my jeans from yesterday, though Georgie did get me a Dolphins T-shirt from the hospital gift shop. My shirt got trashed by the bullet and the paramedics. Thank god I had on that freaking vest. It had been a last minute decision to put it on.

"Ladies, here you go." Sam comes up beside us, looking flushed and sweaty.

"Thanks, honey." Georgie gets on her tiptoes and pecks him on the lips. "Is everything okay?"

"Fine." He runs a hand over the top of his thick dark hair. "I've just had more of a challenge with the event organizers than I thought. They keep allowing people in through the side door because their costumes won't fit through the main entrance."

I crinkle my nose. "That's not good." It means they're not going through security.

He adds, "A party of five just came in dressed as a walrus."

"You mean all five?" Georgie asks.

"Yeah." Sam doesn't sound amused. "It was a lot of work frisking them."

"I definitely need to get in there and see this." Georgie claps excitedly.

Sam's silvery eyes glitter with disapproval.

"Not that we're staying long," I say to placate

him. "I'm still in yesterday's clothes, and I need a shower." My hair is pulled back into a ponytail, but I look like hell.

"It's fine," he says with a tired sigh. "Stay as long as you like. It's safe. Otherwise, I wouldn't let Georgie near this place."

"Oh. Okay." His assurance actually makes me feel better. Now all I have to do is pull Mitch aside and ask him point blank, *How do you feel about me?*

"I gotta go and keep an eye on the large aquatic sea creatures." Sam gives Georgie a peck and runs off.

"Abi, love!"

I turn my head to see none other than Leland Merrick in a wetsuit. The type with the short sleeves and legs.

"Leland." I offer him a tight smile. "Didn't expect to see you here. And what are you dressed as?"

"Sexy." He flashes a charming grin and turns his attention to Georgie. "Miss Walton, such a pleasure to meet the famous heiress who helped bring down her own father." He leans in. "Any chance of getting an interview? We could do a full two-hour special."

"Uh, no." She looks at me. "See you inside, Abi."

"Leland, what do you want?" I growl.

"We had a deal, love. And if I recall, I gave you lots of scratches, but here I am, all itchy."

I roll my eyes. "Sorry. But I'm sure you saw that Mitch went public, so the scoop is gone."

He leans in to whisper in my ear, "Oh no, doll, it's just heating up. And I want an exclusive with Mitch."

"Sorry. Can't help you there. Besides, if you've ever met Mitch, he kinda has a mind of his own. I wouldn't be able to pull any strings for you."

"Fair enough. But tell him the Kemmlers have already agreed to talk to me and tell their side of the story. They're refuting everything."

I lift a brow. "Were you expecting them to come out and say that Grandpa Ralf *was* a war criminal?"

"No, love. They fessed up to that little morsel. I'm talking about the hit on Mitch. They claim, vociferously, that they would never do such a thing."

I shrug. "I'm not surprised." They have a lot to lose, and considering their underhanded behavior, I wouldn't expect them to just come out and say, "Oh garsh! Ya caught me."

"Unless Kristoff decides to turn against his employer, then I'm afraid there's no proof that the Kemmlers broke any laws, which means the crime will be tried in a court of public opinion." Leland whips out a card. From where? I don't know. The suit is skintight. I can see the outline of his strong biceps, pecs, and oh! And *that*, too.

Leland goes on, "Tell Mitch if he wants his story told properly, he'd better call—"

"Me!" The tall brunette from the fundraiser the other night jumps out of nowhere and snatches the card right from Leland's hand. "You tell Mitch that this crusty old crumpet can't be trusted." She pushes her card in my hand. "But I can. I'll make sure the interview isn't edited to make him look like a paranoid asshole."

"Gisselle," Leland snarls, "what are you doing here?"

She smiles like she wants to bite off Leland's face. "It's a free country."

"I'm referring to the fact that I—"

"Anonymously reported me to Homeland Security so they'd detain me at the airport?" She crosses her arms. "Ha. Nice try, buddy." She pokes him in the chest. "But you didn't do your research—like usual. My brother happens to work for them and guess what? There'll be a nice surprise waiting if you get anywhere near a plane, boat, or train. Can you say 'terrorist watch list'?"

"You evil twat." He narrows his dark eyes.

"Useless knob," she fires back.

"You get me off that list right now," Leland demands. "My mum's birthday is next week, and I was planning to surprise her."

"Well," Gisselle replies, a gleam of satisfaction in her eyes, "I'm sure she's used to being disappointed. She is your mother, after all."

I stand there watching these two rival reporters throw verbal mud pies at each other in the most hilarious pissing match ever. The weird thing is, I think they actually *like* each other. I could swear their faces are filled with the need for hate sex.

I quickly think of Mitch. Even when I loathed him, I still wanted him. Just a little. Which only made me hate him more.

I pat the woman, Gisselle, on the arm. "Good luck. You're going to need it." I head into the venue, hearing loud music coming from inside. The show must be starting.

"Have Mitch call me!" Gisselle screams. "I won't screw him over. I promise."

I offer a polite smile, but I am not about to make promises on behalf of Mitch. He and I don't have that type of relationship. In fact, I have absolutely no idea where we stand. There was this moment after I prevented him from turning into a chlorinated dumpling that Mitch showed me the guy I almost fell for that night at his housewarming party—charming, genuine, and unapologetically confident. But not in a cocky way that says, "Hey, look at me! I have a giant chip on my shoulder." No, this was that other kind of confidence—when a person is happy, loves life, and likes themselves so dang much that they just don't care what anyone thinks. They're not ashamed to be vulnerable or show who they are. They aren't afraid to laugh at themselves. They treat others with respect. For six hours, that was the Mitch I got to know, and last night he returned for a few short minutes.

Now I don't know who I'll find. Good Mitch? Prick Mitch? A sandwich? Okay, that last one was lame, but sandwich Mitch is somewhere in between. He offers to make you a turkey and cheese with mayo in the middle of the night when you've decimated his delicious-looking Italian sub.

I can live with sandwich Mitch. I can definitely live with good Mitch. I cannot live with pooker Mitch. *First things first, Abi. You gotta find out if he even wants you.*

I weave through the very excited, very oddly dressed crowd and find a spot for a shorty like me toward the front. Male models, toting generous phallic packages with extreme padding, strut the catwalk. They are all wearing various distasteful and/or shocking swimsuits. One guy just has a spatula glued to his cock and two plastic eggs—sunny-side up—stuck to his buns.

"Jesus. I'm surprised this company lasted more than one season." I look to my right and spot Georgie, who's standing next to the walrus—party of five!—with a look of utter disbelief.

I sidestep over to her, careful not to disturb the rare species of ocean life. "Hey. Are you thinking what I'm thinking?" I yell into her ear. The music, some hyper-tempo version of "Ocean Man" by a group called Ween, is thumping so loud, the walls are vibrating. I only know the song's name because there's a screen behind the catwalk displaying the title along with the music video, which is really just a compilation from the *Creature from the Black Lagoon* movie.

This is one funky-ass fashion show.

"Hey. You here alone?" a deep voice yells right into my ear.

Startled, I jump to the side, almost knocking Georgie over. *Oh, Jesus!* It's the dolphin from the fundraiser.

"Sorry! I'm with someone."

"Okay, but just so you know, I mate for life." He makes a little dolphin cackle.

"Not. Happening," I sneer.

He bows his pointy head and shrinks back into the densely packed crowd. The event feels more like a rock concert than one of those fancy fashion shows you see on TV where everyone's seated.

The male models just keep on coming, one ridiculous swimsuit after another—a bikini with a harpoon shape on the front for the penis, faux-seal-fur short-shorts, a pair of lederhosen with a thong in the back.

Jesus. I want to meet the men who wear this stuff to the beach. Or maybe that's the problem; they don't exist.

Suddenly, the lights go dark, and the entire room pauses with bated breath. The lights return like an explosion—flashes of white, colors bouncing off every surface, and a strobe effect.

The audience goes wild.

Mitch is standing at the far end of the catwalk, wearing what can only be described as a bowling ball bag. I mean, literally, it's a man's bikini with a little bag stuck to the front. There's a tiny handle and everything.

What in the world?

"I can't believe Mitch is wearing that," screams Georgie. "It's hideous!"

"Affirmative." Yet I can't take my eyes away. Mitch is smiling, chuckling, raising his brawny arms in the air, and having a damned good time. His skin is tan; his abs, thighs, pecs, arms, and legs are ripped. He is Mr. I Don't Give a Fuck slash Let's Have a Laugh.

And I do. His trunks are freakin' hysterical. But the moment he shows the audience that there's a zipper at the top of the bag, the room goes apeshit.

"No. No. Please do not tell me that the bag opens." Georgie can't hear me, but even if she could, I doubt she'd respond. Her gaping mouth and wide eyes say it all. She cannot believe what he's about to do. Neither can I.

Oh God, Mitch. Please don't. Please don't... Like the biggest tease ever, he slowly tugs on the zipper, bringing it completely around the circumference of his package while holding the front flap in place with the other hand.

"You want this?" he yells. "You want to see what's inside?"

A group of ladies behind me start screaming, "Show us your magic spitting cobra, Mitch! Give us a look!"

I cover my face. I've seen him nude. But this is

not an image I want haunting my mind for the rest of my life. In fact, I want to punch him right in the bowling balls because, well…

Fuck. I don't know.

All I can say is that in this moment, I am fighting with everything I've got. I want to body check him and stop this. I don't want the entire world (because we all know this is definitely going viral) seeing my man.

Or future man? Man I want?

Mitch suddenly drops the flap. I gasp and try not to look, but the reaction of the crowd makes it impossible. They're laughing hysterically and booing, but in a playful way.

I have to look. I have to! I spread my fingers and discover that underneath is a layer of fabric with a bunch of bowling pins.

Oh. You sneaky devil.

I fume, but I smile. I can't say I ever imagined this fourth version of Mitch—the sexy fun guy charming the pants off the crowd. No. Really. Some woman just removed her pants and threw them at him.

I shake my head. Next thing I know, the people behind me are pushing me forward, and Mitch is pointing at me and instructing the crowd to help me up.

"Wait. What?" I make the international symbol of ohellno by waving my hands, but no one seems to care. Even Georgie gets in on it.

Defeated and horrified, I stand next to Mitch as he points down at the top of my head. The audience cheers.

I'm going to have a panic attack. It's one thing to want to be extroverted, and it's another to actually be it. I am not. In fact, this is my worst nightmare. I have a very real fear of standing in front of a crowd. *Oh God. Oh God. I'm going to faint.*

Mitch does the time-out signal with his hands, and within a few seconds the music stops.

"Mates!" Mitch calls out to quiet the screaming. "Mates, just a moment of your attention, please!" The room quiets and Mitch is looking at me like he's absolutely and utterly glowing.

Oh God. Is he going to…? Since I was little, I dreamed of something like this. I'm standing in the crowd—not in front of it but *in*—at a big movie premiere. Photographers are lighting up the sky with their flashes, fans are holding signs and yelling words of adoration, the movie stars are glamorous and waving their manicured nails. Suddenly, the last limo pulls up. Everyone falls silent as the hottest man in the world exits the vehicle. For the record, the man has been a different guy at various times of my life. There was Zac Efron, Channing Tatum, Liam Hemsworth, Taylor Lautner, and Nick Jonas, to name a few. These last few years, as I've gotten older, I've been fantasizing about men who are more than just their good looks. Mature men. Responsible men. Men with purpose.

Okay. Yes, sometimes he's Mr. Clean. What woman doesn't want a guy who loves a spotless house? But right now, that man is Mitch. And more than anything, I am hoping that he feels something for me, too. I'm hoping that's why he brought me up here.

"Everyone," he says, "I just wanted to say three things. One, thank you for the support and enthusiasm these past few years. It's been an honor to come to these shows and witness your enthusiasm for me and the Weeno brand. Two," he holds up two fingers, "it is with extreme sadness that I confirm this is my last day as the Weeno ambassador."

Whats and oh nos erupt in the room.

"And third," he turns toward me, "I wanted to leave you all with this: a statement from my heart. A person's greatness and worth isn't about the size of their melons or mighty dangler. It's not about the hardness of your abs."

"Yes, it is, you sexy thing! We love you, Mitch," yells a woman.

"Thank you. Thank you." He smiles and dips his head in gratitude. "But greatness really comes from right here." He looks at me, but places one hand over his heart. "This woman took a bullet for me last night. She stopped two other attempts on my life. She is the best bloody bodyguard—male, female, or otherwise—anyone could ask for. So tonight, Abi Carter, I give you the Weeno Award."

Huh? I'm so confused. The moment went from

heading in a romantic direction to…a Weeno Award?

I don't even know what that is. And more importantly, I don't want to.

Two women come out on the catwalk with a crown that's shaped like an upside-down pair of men's bikini bottoms covered in gold rhinestones. In slow motion, I see the photographers snapping off their pictures. Everyone's pointing and laughing hysterically at me. It's like the scene right out of *Carrie*, but without the blood. Still, the horror! From this day forward, anyone who Googles "Abigail Carter" will find a picture of me wearing Elton John's underpants on my head.

"Stop!" I hold out my hand. "Don't you come near me."

A shock wave of confused faces floods the room.

"Abi? What's wrong?" Mitch asks.

"Is this some joke to you? Am I some joke?" I grab the stupid knicker-crown from the girl's hand and throw it to the ground.

"No. Not at all." Mitch shakes his head.

"Then what the hell, Mitch?" I tear up, feeling too emotional to hold back. Maybe it's the pain in my chest, the lack of sleep, or the stress of facing death, all finally catching up. I don't know. But this is not okay.

"Abi, I just wanted to—"

"Humiliate me? Minimize what I went through? I'm your bodyguard, Mitch. Your *fucking* bodyguard. Not your PR tool, toy, or mate. I took this irreplaceable temple," I sweep my hands over my body, "and used it to shield you and your giant male ego. It's a damned miracle you're still alive because it would take ten of me to cover all of it."

"Abi," he says like he's shocked or perturbed by my words. In either case, he doesn't get it.

"I'm special, Mitch." I point a finger in his face. "And for whatever reason, I felt like you were worth giving my life for. But I'll be damned if I let you thank me by putting underwear on my head." Somewhere deep inside, I'm realizing that my anger is about more than that. The truth is, I saved his life and it wasn't about the money. I did it because I cared what happened to Mitch. A part of me just can't get over him, so maybe all this fighting for his life has really been about fighting for us.

Or my hope for us?

I don't know.

All I can say is that he drives me crazy. He walks into a room and my heart fires up. My stomach knots. My head spins. All this time I've spent feeling angry, I was secretly hoping he wanted me as much as I want him, as much as he wanted me that night.

Clearly he doesn't. He's all about the fame, the glory, and his swimming career. I'm a joke to him. *Stupid! Stupid, Abi! Why do you set yourself up like this?*

"Let's go backstage, Abi. Let's talk this out," Mitch says.

"I gotta go." I head straight down the catwalk, through the backstage area, and out the walrus exit. I don't stop until I'm on my way to the airport.

> ***Georgie:*** *Abi, you okay?*
>
> ***Me:*** *Sure. Peachy. Enjoy the rest of the weekend with Sam. See you back in Houston.*

CHAPTER SEVENTEEN

MITCH

That didn't go at all how I imagined. I scratch my scruffy chin, trying to comprehend how my gesture toward Abi turned into a festering dung heap.

I look down at the crowd, who's still standing there staring at me.

"Well, uh," I scratch the back of my head, "that was a bit awkward, but I hope you all enjoy the rest of your evening. Swim on!" I signal to the bloke in the DJ booth to spin some music. I walk backstage and spot Norton, the owner of Weeno, surrounded by reporters.

At least one person's happy about all that. Weeno is going to get a boatload of free publicity and social media buzz from that debacle.

"You've done some stupid things, buddy, but this takes the cake." Sam stifles a smile, meeting me just outside my changing room.

"Right. Thanks, Sam." *Ass.*

"Sorry, sorry." He turns serious on me. "It's just that you tried to put underwear on her head. As a thank-you."

"They were swimmers. Shiny ones. And I was attempting to be nice."

"I thought you had experience with women."

Little known fact: I have never had a serious girlfriend. Yeah, I've slept with a few. I partied a lot in my late teens and early twenties, but swimming has always been my girl. And she leaves me no time to be unfaithful.

I shrug. "Sure."

"Then maybe you need a refresher, *mate*," he says, mocking my accent. "Because that girl is in love with you."

Abi. In love with me? "You've lost your marbles there, Sam, because that woman hates my guts." Sure, she said something about falling in love with me right before Ash showed up, but she was joking. And yes, she let me kiss her before it all went down. Heat of the moment and all that. But after the crap I've pulled, the things I've said, the danger I put her in, how could she be falling for a man like me? To entertain the thought is a joke, even if a day hasn't gone by where I don't think of her. Her golden brown eyes, her sweet smile, and that soft little body. Hands down, she's the smartest, bravest, sexiest woman I've ever met.

"Mitch, I only know two women in my life who'd jump in front of a bullet for me without thinking. My mother and Georgie. Abi has saved your ass twice."

"Three. There was the power cord in the swimming pool incident."

Sam cocks a brow. "You and I need to have better communication. But, fine. Three incidents, which only proves my point. She loves you. She might not want to admit it, but she does."

I whoosh out a breath and run a hand through my hair. "Dammit." He has a point. And here I am, treating her like one of my mates. "Are you sure? Because you'd think a strongheaded, mouthy girl like that would just come out and say how she feels." If she really feels it.

"I'm sure that's what you're used to, Mitch; women falling at your feet and declaring their undying love. But Abi isn't like that. She's actually pretty shy."

Abi? "If that's true, she doesn't have issues speaking up to me." She seems to enjoy pushing my buttons.

"Trust me. Georgie and Abi have been best friends since they were kids, and I've gotten to know her. She's proud, hardworking, and very loyal. But deep down, she's not as tough as she seems."

I remember Abi mentioning that she was terminally shy growing up, which was why they gave her the sarcastic nickname of Blabi, but I thought she was exaggerating. "Does this mean it was a mistake putting her up on stage?"

Sam points his index finger and clicks with his mouth. "Now you're catching on, Weeno boy. Let's get out of here."

I narrow my eyes. "You keep away from me and my Weeno, shrimpy."

"Very fucking funny, Mitch. Now please get out of that oh-so-manly thong so we can get out of here."

I turn, making a production of sticking out my ass.

"Stop it. Or I swear the next bullet will be yours."

I laugh and go into my dressing room, but the moment I'm alone, Sam's words start to sink in. Really sink in. If Abi loves me, then what do I do about it? I've never had a real relationship for damned good reason. I don't want one and I don't have time.

As for Abi, the decent man in me says she deserves someone who's all in—gold medals, perfect strokes, tireless execution in the relationship department. I am a competitive person who'd want to be there for his woman in every way possible—friendship, support, incredible sex. More incredible sex. But I'm not capable of dedicating myself to anything but my sport. It's been my life. It's kept me sane in my darkest hours. It's given me purpose. *And more importantly, swimming can't die.* I don't have to worry about being unable to protect it because some fucking psycho is after me. I don't have to spend every waking minute wondering what I could have done differently to save it. I don't have nightmares about watching it bleed out in my driveway while I plead with God to take my life instead. I've lost my entire family—parents, grandparents, and uncle—which is why no matter how much I want Abi, I can't do right by her. I'll never allow myself to love her fully like she deserves. Especially now, after she almost died yesterday. That image will haunt me until the day I die.

If I care for this amazing woman, I will let her go. Again.

CHAPTER EIGHTEEN

ABI

It's been almost a week since Miami, and I cannot believe the crap I've had to put up with. *Memes? Seriously, people? You just had to create little cartoony stories about me for sharing with the world?*

Overnight, I've become the Weenonator. Yeah, that's right. The Terminator of Weeno. Apparently, my reaction to the Weeno Award has become a symbol for the rejection of "toxic masculinity" on "insightful" journalistic websites such as MenAreFartBags.com, IHateAnythingWithaDick.net and DieMen!Die.org.

I can't even…

I don't know what's worse; the fact that Mitch did that to me, when I was starting to have feelings for him, or that the poor Weeno company is getting hammered over my rejection of their man-panty crown. Either way, it's a disaster and I need to get back to work.

Unfortunately, Sam has been avoiding me. After texting him for the eighth time in three days, I finally call him, as Georgie so delicately hinted I should do—*Pick up your phone and call, Abi! Or I swear I'll divorce you both!*

P.S. I know I'm not married to Sam yet, but I will take action if the two of you don't talk.

"Hey, Abi, how are you?" Sam answers his phone sounding like a doctor who's about to deliver very bad news.

"Am I fired?"

"How did you know?" he replies.

"It's a little obvious, don't you think?"

"Listen, Abi. I think you're incredible. In fact, the best bodyguard I've ever seen, but—"

"But 'you're fired'? Seriously, Sam?"

"No. And yes."

I hang my head. "Why? What did I do?"

"This is not your calling. I want it to be. You'd be a huge asset to my company. But this isn't you."

"Why would you say that when I kept your biggest client alive? Okay, it was less than a week, but that was a tough few days! Like, dog-year days."

"Your skills aren't in question, Abi. You could do this job with your arms tied behind your back. But this isn't what you really want, is it?"

"Well…"

"It's okay to say the truth."

"I wanted it for now. Doesn't that count?"

"Abi!" Georgie comes on the phone. "Here's the sitch, 'kay? I'm giving you the money to finish school. Your mom has already decided she's selling the house and will use the money for a start-up and to pay her legal bills."

I roll my eyes. "I'm not taking your money, Georgie."

"Uh. Ya. You totally are."

"No. I'm not." She can't see me, but I stomp a foot anyway.

"Yes, you are, and if you don't—"

"Abi," Sam is now back on, "Georgie considers you a sister, and that means so do I. So while we might not be the family you were born with, we are the family you've chosen. So, I beg you—something I never do because it offends my male senses—to take the money and let us all get a good night's sleep."

Ugh…I don't want to. I can't. I'm not about handouts. "Sam, Georgie, I appreciate the gesture, but—"

"It's not a gift, Abi," Sam cuts in. "You earned it. As part of the SMS family and the extraordinary service you've given to our gold-star client, I am giving you a bonus of fifty thousand dollars. Do what you like with it, but the money is already in your account."

I'm defeated. And while my pride protests, my heart doesn't. It means a lot to me that Sam and Georgie would help me like this. "Thank you, guys. I really mean it."

"We love you, Abi. And we just hope you'll remember that when we ask for free, unlimited babysitting in about seven months."

"What!"

Georgie giggles. "Surprise, Auntie Abi!"

"What? Ohmygod. Congratulations!" The wedding is set for June, so Georgie is going to need a different dress. The one she picked out had a tight corseted waist.

"I know. I'm a soiled, indecent woman. But man, is Sam's baby hammer powerful. He just pounded that sperm right in there."

I cringe. "And…we'll be ending the conversation right here. Congratulations. Thank you for firing me, Sam. I mean it. We'll talk soon."

"Oh. Don't hang up!" Georgie yells as I pull the phone from my ear. "We need to talk about Mi—"

"I love you! Buh-bye." I end the call quickly. The last thing in the world I want is to talk about Mitch. For my own sanity, I'm done with him. And shame on me for letting the fantasy in my head get so big that it took on a life of its own.

My phone chirps, and I answer, "Georgie, I'm serious. I don't want to talk about—"

"This isn't Georgie. It's Gisselle Walters."

The reporter woman? "How'd you get this number?"

"I have my ways."

"Okay. Well, I have things to do, so—"

"How do you feel about the news that Kristoff Bones has escaped?"

"Sorry? When did this happen?"

"The news just hit a few hours ago. He took out three guards while in transit to another jail."

Fuck. "But they'll catch him before he goes anywhere, right?"

"Who knows. The man is the master of disguise, a world-class hit man."

"You think he's coming here to Houston?"

"If there's money in it."

"Is there?" Because I remember Georgie mentioning that was over. The Kemmlers wouldn't dare go after Mitch now.

"Can I get a quote? I need it for my story."

"Yes. Goodbye—you can quote me on that."

I quickly dial back Georgie.

"Hello?"

"Why didn't you tell me that crazy Kristoff broke free?" I bark.

"I tried. Remember? You hung up."

"What happens next?" My heart starts to pound.

"That's what I was trying to tell you. Sam wanted to reassure you that this Kristoff guy is halfway around the planet. They'll catch him before he gets anywhere near Mitch, but as an extra safety precaution, Sam found a new owl, so you have nothing to worry about. Mitch will be kept safe."

"Oh, well…it's not like I care. I just wanted to be sure you knew about it."

"Uh-huh. Sure…"

"So, um…who's the new owl?" I don't even

know why I'm asking. It's not like I'm jealous or anything.

"I don't know. Just some woman. Sam says she's got solid military training and blends right into the detail."

I am *not* jealous. He is *not* my man to protect. He is *not* mine at all. "Great. Sounds great."

"Hey, Abi?"

"Yeah?"

"I know it's over between you and Mitch—"

"Never even started," I correct.

"Okay. If you say so. But he has some big national time trial thing this afternoon at the university. I'm going, if you wanted to come and keep me company?"

I suddenly hear retching on the other end of the phone.

"G-cow? Are you okay?"

She hacks and then comes back on. "Oh wow. That was nasty."

"You have morning sickness?" I ask.

"Morning? I should be so lucky. I'm pretty much talking to the monster all day long. Ralfff...yack."

Poor thing. I can't imagine being sick the entire day. "Where's Sam?"

"He just left for work. But don't worry. I'm fine. A few crackers and some—oh, hold on! I need to blow a few more chunks." She heaves in the background. "And...that was part of my stomach."

"You should stay home and rest. Not go to some swim meet."

"I'm not staying cooped up for the next seven months—or however long this lasts. No way. Because once my little nipple-nibbler shows up, my days of freedom are toast. But don't worry about me. I'll be fine." She sighs. "All alone. With my barf bag. Sitting in the bleachers while Sam guards Mitch."

"A, you're the worst." She knows exactly how to push my protective buttons. "B, why don't you just come here? We can watch movies and eat pop-corn—"

More heaving. "Don't say that word, Abi. Not if you want to live."

"You weren't this sick in Miami."

"My mom says it's the Walton curse. Starting in the second month, we get extreme vomiting or monster hemorrhoids. Trust me, I'll take vomiting over elephantiasis of the butthole any day. My pants would fit all weird."

Eeesh.

"Anyway, the only thing that seems to help is fresh air," she adds, "but I totally understand if you don't want to come because one of the swimmers just happens to be some guy you don't even care about."

Damn her. "I hate you."

"See you there at two?"

"Yep." I sigh. "But I'm closing my eyes when he

swims, and I am not going to speak to him. Got it? Because if you so much as make me try, I will spread evil rumors about you. That reporter lady, Gisselle Whatsherface, is dying for an exclusive, and I think I can come up with one: Georgie Walton has secret love child with Weeno walrus."

"That actually has a nice ring to it." She snickers.

"Shut up."

"See you there. I gotta go. The porcelain god demands many sacrifices in his honor, and I must obey."

We end the call, and I just want to scream. I'm not stupid. I know why Georgie is doing this. She hopes Mitch and I might work it out because, let's face it, she fan girls over him. But as much as I love her, I can't give her what she wants. Mitch doesn't care about me or anything but himself and swimming. Proof being that whole fashion shit-show and the fact that he's made zero effort to make amends—even as friends—for his incredibly insensitive gesture.

Of course, I have no one to blame but myself. It was stupid of me to build up our connection into this immature romantic fantasy.

Maybe after today, Georgie will see I'm right. She'll see that Mitch loves his fame and career more than any human being. He won't even notice I'm there.

CHAPTER NINETEEN

MITCH

Fuck. She brought Abi? And they're sitting in the front row? Why the bloody hell would she do that? I've already told Sam, which is the same as telling Georgie since those two are thick as thieves, that I don't want to see her. Yes, I could have handled things differently when showing my appreciation for all that she's done. Yes, I find her incredibly attractive and think about her every minute of the goddamned day. But it will pass. It has to. I can't give her what she deserves, and if I tried, I'd only end up breaking her heart. *I love only one woman and she's fifty by twenty-five meters.*

I do my stretches at the far end of the pool, where only athletes, coaches, and the event staff are allowed. It's a cold day here in Houston, definitely not what I'm used to coming from the southern hemisphere, where the temperatures are warmer in February, but the pool is heated, and if I want to put Texas U firmly on the map, then I need a national title under my belt. After the 2020 Olympics, and winning four more medals, my plan is to make this university a world-class training facility, which I will lead. That's my goal. It's why I took Texas U's offer to train here even though I'm still swimming for Australia in Tokyo.

I keep my back to the photographers positioned around the sides of the pool and the spectators at the far end. Sam and his team of three lurk in the background, including my new Abi—a woman old enough to be my granny. In fact, that's exactly what she's posing as. An idea Sam got from the fundraiser. Guillotine granny had flown under everyone's radar and likely wouldn't have been caught if it hadn't been for Abi's keen owl eyes.

Abi. Don't think about her. Don't think about…

"Swimmers to your mark," the announcer calls.

I take my position on the number ten diving block and put on my goggles. My mind automatically does what it's been trained to do. Thousands of miles. Hundreds of thousands of hours. I don't need to wish for a victory, I just need to have confidence that it's there. I've done the work. My body knows what to do.

Suddenly, the world around me falls away. I see the turquoise blue water, the lanes, and the finish line. I see myself three body lengths ahead as I touch that wall. There is no doubt in my mind. *There is only me. Winning. There is only me. Winning. There is only—*

I glance up across the pool and my focus is shattered. Abi. She's watching me with a huge frown.

"Beep!"

Oh shit! Startled by the sound, I dive into the water, but fuck me, I'm already a second behind. *Focus. Focus. Focus. Why the hell were you thinking about her? Dammit, I'm still thinking about her! Stop it.*

One. Two. One. Two. One. Two. Breathe. One. Two. I try to find my rhythm, but my mind is playing a game of tug-o-war. The sheer act of trying not to think about Abi is only making me think about her more.

For the first time in my life, I am going to lose a race. Maybe I deserve it.

I push my head to the side and take a breath. It's only a split-second view, but I realize I've been psyching myself out. There's no one beside me, and I have a full view of the other lanes. I'm sure as hell not behind anyone. Even on my worst day, I'm faster than most. If I were in jeopardy of losing, the other swimmer would be in my line of sight.

I find my stride and effortlessly glide through the water. I'm at one with it. It's as natural as a dolphin slipping through the waves.

That's it, mate, I tell myself. Just do what you were born to do.

The wall is eight strokes away. Knowing I'll have to do my turn, I pull hard and take a breath. But when I look to the spot where my eyes naturally gravitate, I see something that makes me stop.

ABI

Wow. Okay. I now get why Mitch is a world champion. He got off to a bumpy start, which I suspect isn't his usual routine, but within a few seconds, he's pulled ahead by at least five feet. I can't explain it, but watching him move is like watching a bird fly. He's effortless and graceful.

Not that this changes anything about the way I feel about him.

"Go, Mitch! Woo-hoo!" Georgie yells from our seats in the front row. And what d' ya know. She's been gobbling down nuts, fruit, and other snacks since we arrived.

I've been bamboozled. It almost makes me sad because it shows how desperately she wants me to find love. As much as I want it, too, I have to accept that I won't find it with Mitch. Doesn't matter that I felt this incredible connection with him that I haven't felt with any other man. Doesn't matter that being around him makes my heart beat faster or my lips tingle. Yes. Both sets. Doesn't matter how much his smile makes me want to spend the rest of my life discovering ways to make him do it as much as possible. I have to let him go.

The seconds fly, and just when Mitch is about to do his turn, he halts.

Huh? Why is he stopping? The other swimmers do that flip and twist thing and head in the opposite direction while Mitch is suddenly out of the pool, coming straight for me. The crowd around us in the front row of the bleachers is frozen, wondering what the hell is going on. It all happens so fast—Mitch pulling back his fist, that large bicep flexing, the entire arm flying toward my face. I want to duck. I know I should, but my brain is at a stalemate. Why is he about to punch me? *Does not compute. Does not compute!*

His powerful fist flies through the air, whizzing past my ear, and I hear a *smack!* Like someone punching a side of beef. A loud grunt is followed by screams and gasps.

I turn my head and the guy behind me has a vacant look in his eyes. I can almost see the stars circling his head.

The man goes cross-eyed and falls backward into a woman's lap.

Mitch cranks back the old fist again, ready to give him another.

"Mitch!" Georgie pushes out her hands. "Stop. What are you doing?"

An older woman, with gray hair and blue eyes, is jumping between Mitch and me, shielding him with her body. Phil pops out of nowhere, jumping on top of the guy.

"He has a knife!" Mitch yells. "He was going to stab her!"

Sam shows up, pulling Georgie away. Phil starts dragging the man, who's out cold, down to the ground.

My head is about to explode. Chaos erupts as onlookers don't know if this is a gun situation, a terrorist bomb threat, or what. The only people stepping closer are the film crews from the sports channels.

Phil checks the man's breathing and then pulls something from his hand. He stares down at it like he's genuinely confused.

"What is it?" Sam barks.

Phil hesitantly produces a butter knife. There's a block of cheese on the ground.

"What the?" From the look in Mitch's hazel eyes, this cheese knife comes as a surprise.

"What did you do to my husband! Ohmygod! Eddie!" A woman rushes to the unconscious man. She's holding a paper plate in her hand. "I just went to the car for a minute! What did you do to him?" She looks at the faces around her, but only one person hangs his head.

Mitch runs a strong hand through his dripping hair. "I saw the reflection of the metal. He was holding it inward, like he was about to stab her." Mitch looks at me, and I see the humiliation in his eyes. "I thought it was some kind of retaliation."

Oh God. Poor guy. The devastation is more than I can stomach.

I get up and take his hand. "Come on. Let's get you to the locker room." I lead him away. "It's okay, Mitch. He'll be fine."

"I assaulted a spectator. I blew my heat. I'm finished."

I can't say anything because I don't know squat about the rules. All I can say is that had the butter-knife man been after more than just a slice of cheese for his poolside picnic, it's nice to know Mitch would have had my back.

CHAPTER TWENTY

We enter Mitch's house, and this is the first time I've genuinely felt like I can't be anywhere near him. My body gets all fluttery and hot. My heart wants so badly for him and me to happen. I have the biggest, baddest case of heart throbs for this man, but I refuse to let myself go there. There being that place where I start hoping again.

"Okay. So…Phil and Igor are outside, your nanny is in the kitchen making you a snack, so I'm gonna head home. Just be sure not to turn on the TV."

Everything's settled with the police, and the man at the pool said he wouldn't be pressing charges, but I know the press will be relentless. They're always itching to vilify people, like bullies on a playground who've been given megaphones.

"I'm gonna head out." I point to the door as Mitch takes a seat in his private living room. He's wearing a black warm-up suit, and his face is ghost white, matching the rugs.

"Hey. You'll be okay," I say. "This will all blow

over."

"I'm done." He stares at the wall. "It's over. Just like that—a lifetime career is thrown away."

"I think you're just in shock. Give it time. The dust will settle and you can relook at your options. I mean, there will always be more competitions."

"No. Not for me. This was it." He shakes his head.

"But you're only twenty-seven and—"

"Twenty-six. I'm twenty-six. And I'm going to be suspended. Maybe a year. Maybe for life. Either way, I'm out of the running for the Olympics."

"Oh." I take a seat next to him and place my hand over his. "I had no idea. This is awful." If only I'd stayed home. If only I hadn't let Georgie guilt me into going. "I know you really wanted one more shot at those gold medals. I'm so, so sorry, Mitch."

He says nothing for several long moments. "I'm not. Not even a little."

I crane my neck to see his face. Even with both of us seated, he towers over me. "Sorry?"

"I'm glad it's over."

"Errr…but you live to swim. You've put your entire life into it."

"I know." He runs his hand through his thick brown hair. "I fully believed that man wanted to hurt you. I didn't know why. I didn't care why. I thought I was going to watch you die."

"I'm still not following."

"After Miami, I was pissed at you for jumping

in front of that bullet. I told myself it was because I wasn't worth dying for, but really, I hated feeling so goddamned helpless. I remember losing both my parents to illness when I was little. I watched my uncle die. And here you come along to remind me I can't do shit to save anyone, not even myself. Today reminded me that I am a fighter. I am willing to do whatever it takes to protect what I love."

I tilt my head. Because it almost sounds like he's trying to say… *No. No. I refuse to go there.* "What's your point?"

He turns his entire body to face me. "Do you have any idea how much I've wanted you? How hard it's been to stay away?"

I shake my head slowly, but I don't speak. I'm unsure if he's really saying what I'm hearing.

He continues, "I would rather spend the rest of my life loving you and missing you than know I never had the balls to love you at all. Which is what I've been doing, pushing you away and putting swimming first."

"And now? Are you saying I'd come first?" It's hard to believe from what I've seen.

"Yes. You will come first. And more importantly, it's what I want."

I swallow a weird lump in my throat. "You want to give up swimming? For me?"

"No. And yes."

I lift two brows.

"I don't want to give up swimming. And I

won't. I'll keep doing it like I always planned—coaching, helping others achieve their dreams. But I want you more than I want anything else."

"Why?" I ask, because it all feels so sudden.

"Abi," he cups the back of my neck, "because I'd take our future, the potential of us for the next fifty, sixty, whatever years, over another four gold medals any day."

I blink at him, pushing back the tears. This is not the declaration of love I dreamed of since I was a little girl, it's a thousand times better.

Our eyes lock, and he leans in to kiss me, but stops short. "Oh, and Abi?"

"Yes?"

"Before I forget, thank you for saving my life. And I'm not just talking about the bullet you took. Or the power cord. Or the giant-knife-wielding senior citizen."

I smile, and it comes from the deepest part of my happy soul. "You're welcome."

He kisses me, and it feels like magic on my lips. Love, coated in destiny and filled with the profoundest desire.

The warmth of his mouth quickly spreads through my body.

He pulls away, and we lock eyes again. I could stare at the green, golds, and yellows all day long, but more than anything, I love the way he's looking at me. Like there's nowhere he'd rather be and no one else he'd rather be with. *Is this really happening?*

"Can I take you to my room?" he asks. "I really want to finish what we started the night we met."

"Me too." Then again, had we slept together, we might not have arrived at this moment. I'm stronger because of everything I went through. And I now know, without a shadow of a doubt, Mitch will have my back and I'll have his. No matter what.

CHAPTER TWENTY-ONE

MITCH

I carry Abi up to my bedroom, unsure of how to tell her what I'm thinking. It's been a while, a long while, since I've been with a girl.

I hadn't slept with anyone for months before I met her, and I haven't since. I used my training as an excuse. Then my uncle died, and that killed my urges to get close to anyone. *Or maybe I was just waiting for Abi. Maybe she's what I've been looking for all along.*

Whatever the case, she's brought me back to the man I really am. Brave. Willing to fight for what he wants. Confident in his ability to make anything happen. Somewhere along the way, while being hunted like a prized elk, I lost the part of myself that gave a fuck about others. Self-preservation mode.

Yeah, sure. I also didn't want anything interfering with my other woman: swimming. I worked hard to win her approval. I dedicated a good portion of my life to her. And when the most important thing in your life is perfect and makes you happy, you hesitate to ask for something better, something more. It's asking for trouble.

But I remember my uncle once telling me that right now isn't right forever. I think what he meant is that we need different things at different times in our lives. And moving on doesn't signify that those endeavors were a waste of time. No. They were exactly what you needed at that point in your life. What's wrong is not being able to let go. It's hanging onto a dream after its expiration date. It's living in the past.

It took Abi coming along to show me that it was time to find a new dream and step down from the starting block so others can have their moment in the spotlight.

Yeah, I know I could stick with swimming for another few years after my suspension is over, but at what cost? Abi would be long gone, and she's the one I want.

Might seem sudden to anyone looking from the outside in, but to me, love isn't knowing every detail about a person. That's for cowards. It's about knowing enough to make you want to spend the rest of your life pulling back the layers.

I set Abi down at the foot of my bed, already feeling hungry for her. I've visualized this moment hundreds of times. The feel of her soft skin, the taste of her on my mouth, the sound of her soft moans.

She stares up at me with those light brown eyes. "Are you sure, Mitch? This is really what you want?

Because if you're just saying all this to get into my pants, then—"

"I am definitely saying this to get into your pants. But I plan to stay there…forever. Wait. That sounded weird, not at all charming and romantic like I hoped."

She grins, and it's the sort of smile that confirms what's in my heart. I've made the right choice. Because in all my years, no medal has ever made me feel this good.

ABI

I have no words. Here I'd thought that Mitch would be devastated over that mess at today's competition. Instead, it was some sort of epiphany.

I can't lie. His one-eighty leaves me filled with skepticism. I'm not saying he's a liar or playing me right now. But is this, *am I*, really what he wants? All I can say is that once again, I'm willing to take the risk.

Because this guy? Good Mitch? He's worth it. He's the one I want, and if he's real, I'll take him.

Standing at the foot of his bed, he pulls my T-shirt over my head and then unbuttons my pants. I quickly help him out of his clothes.

Unlike me, he's commando, and I find it sexy as hell. That, and he's hard. I remember the feel of him sliding between my thighs, stroking me to the point of ecstasy with the length of his shaft. Now I get the full picture, and it's impressive. Thicker than I can wrap a hand around. Longer than I think my body can accommodate. More sinfully arousing than I imagined.

I remove my bra, and he slowly pushes me back on to the bed. Eager for him, I pull him along by the hand, guiding him on top of me so I can get closer to those lips and the rest of him. His body is warm, but his kisses are hot and ravenous, filled with nips, sucks, and pauses at all the right moments. Our tongues stroke and slide while our bodies grind in a carnal, demanding rhythm. The only thing keeping us separated is my panties, and those are quickly losing their welcome.

His large hands begin to roam and explore, one landing on my breast, where it teases my taut nipple. A little tug, and I'm moaning for something more.

He takes the subtle direction like the pro that he is, and his mouth begins the trek downward, leaving a trail of kisses down my neck and collarbone until he finds my nipple.

He takes my breast and gently squeezes the soft mound, allowing him to bring more of the sensitive flesh inside his mouth. He sucks hard, sparking an intense tingle deep inside my womb. It's deliciously painful, and I want more.

His mouth makes its way to the other breast while his free hand buries itself down the front of my panties.

His movements are sure and skilled because there is no fumbling around. The pad of his thumb presses over my c-spot, and I buck with pleasure, feeling his fingers plunge inside me.

He's not gentle.

In fact, he's rougher than I expected, and I moan from the welcome intrusion.

He breaks the kiss and stops moving his hand, but stays inside me. "Are you all right?"

I nod frantically. "Yes. Better than all right. Don't stop."

"Good. Because I need you ready."

"I'm ready." I slide my hand to the nape of his neck and smash my lips to his, grinding my hips into his hand.

"No," he pants between kisses, "I mean for this." With his free hand, he guides mine down to his solid cock.

Dear God. Did it get bigger? I look down at the gap between our bodies as I stroke the velvety flesh. I'm only able to close my hand around three-quarters of it. The soft head glistens with a bead of cum, and I use the tip of my finger to spread it over the crown in a circular motion. He groans with pleasure, and I answer by pushing my pelvis harder into his hand.

"You feel so good. So wet," he says, his voice husky. "But I don't think you're ready."

"I am. I promise."

No matter how skilled he is, his hand can't relieve the building pressure. I need all of him. I need to feel his thick shaft pushing me to my limits.

He rolls over and reaches into his nightstand. I hear the wrapper tear, and a moment later he's back, settling between my thighs.

He takes my hands and holds them over my head. "Just tell me if you want to stop. Otherwise, I'm just going to fuck the hell out of you."

Uh…sounds good to me? "Okay."

It takes him just a moment to find my slick and ready entrance with the crown of his shaft. I urge him forward with a nudge of my hips.

Slowly, he pushes in just a few inches and pulls out. It's not the hard, animalistic thrust I expected, and I get why. Every inch deeper he goes, I feel my body working to stretch around him. He takes his time, allowing my wetness to coat him and pave the way for deeper penetration.

I relax into it, enjoying every inch of sensation until it's done. He's deep. And it's better than I imagined. My heart is racing a million beats per second, and I will myself not to come as he stays inside but stops moving.

Still pinning my hands over my head, he kisses my neck and lips and shoulder. He waits until I'm greedy for him, writhing beneath him, silently begging for climax.

"Please, please fuck me. Hard." I need him to release this tension. Nothing else matters.

He pulls his lips away and smiles devilishly. "Only because you asked."

His eyes locked with mine, he pulls completely out and then drives hard.

"Ohgod." I gasp with pleasure, feeling him push against my womb and my g-spot. He withdraws and does it again.

"Faster. Now faster," I beg.

I can tell he was holding back before, but with my reassurances, he gives it everything he's got. The penetrations come fast and unrelentingly deep, making me question my own sanity. The pain and pleasure mix into a sinful cocktail of need. I meet him thrust for thrust, enjoying the feel of his balls slapping at the base of my entrance. I look down again at the small space between us as he lifts himself up with his strong arms. His abs ripple in time to his expert hips. His cock guides him to the perfect place each time.

I'm going to come. I don't want to, but I can't help it. He's too fucking sexy. He feels too fucking good inside me. "I'm…I'm…"

He takes my cue and pounds me with merciless strokes. Suddenly, my entire body freezes. I'm outside myself, hearing my moans, but at the same time, my mind is lost inside the waves of pleasure racking every inch of my body. I'm here with him, but I don't know where that is. Pure ecstasy isn't a place. He lets out a deep animalistic growl and joins me as he comes hard. I feel his cock twitch with each euphoric contraction of my walls. I'm desperate for more. I want it to go on and on. I don't want it to ever stop.

A few moments pass, and my orgasm melts away, leaving behind perfectly limp muscles—legs, arms, everything. "Wow. That was…amazing."

"You feel so good, Abi. I don't want to leave your body. Not ever." His mouth returns to mine, administering deep lazy kisses. Still hard as a rock, he slowly moves inside me, triggering those little sparks of sinful contractions.

"I'm a woman. I can keep going if you can." I've never felt this aroused, this hungry for a man. Especially not after coming so hard. But the wetness he brought out is proof of how he sends my body into pleasure overload.

He reaches down and grabs the base of his cock. "Let me just change my con—" He freezes and looks at me.

"What?"

"It broke."

"Sorry?"

"The condom broke." He winces and withdraws.

I look down at what is in fact a very giant cock with a little latex turtleneck around it.

"Ohmygod. What does this mean? What does this mean?"

"Just…stay calm. It's okay. I'm, uh…let me just go take care of this," he points to his broken prophylactic, "and we can…you know. Talk."

I hop from the bed, grab my pants with my cell in the pocket, and rush into his bathroom, cutting in front of him.

"I'll use the bathroom downstairs," he says through the door.

"Oh-okay." I try not to sound frantic, but that's a fail.

I press my back to the door and remind myself to keep breathing. *He didn't inject you with poison, Abi. It was just a boatload of sperm. You won't die. Don't pass out.*

The bathroom is all light gray natural stones with a sauna and dual-headed shower. If I weren't so terrified of doing a face-plant on the floor, I'd be all over that shit.

I pace for several minutes, debating if I should call Georgie.

No. No. That's silly. You're a grown woman. You can deal with this. I start jumping up and down, hoping gravity might lend me a hand. *Goddammit. I bet he's got strong swimmers!* I revert to trying to remember every urban legend, every home remedy, every…

Wait. I'm due for my period like…tomorrow. And mine is an anal-retentive bitch who believes in punctuality. I let out a sigh of relief. As long as he's been safe and taking care of himself, I'll be okay.

I clean up, splash some water on my face, and dry it with a hand towel before grabbing my phone.

The bedroom is empty. “Mitch?”

I wait, but don’t hear anything.

Knowing there are security guards patrolling the property, I grab the robe hanging on the hook in his bathroom. It drags on the floor as I take the stairs. My brain goes into nightmare mode. *I know he said he went to use the other bathroom, but did he just run out on me?*

“Mitch? Mitch? I swear to God. If you’ve just decided this isn’t going to work...” I enter the kitchen and find Mitch standing in a pair of red boxers, doing his very best to remain calm.

A tall man with white hair, whom I’ve never seen before, is standing with a gun pointed at Mitch from across the marble kitchen island.

Oh shit. Oh shit. This time, I’m fresh out of tricks. I have no gun, no vest, and I’m too far away to get that gun from his hands. My only weapon is my brain.

“Uh...excuse me?” I say with as much attitude as I can muster. “But who the *fuck* are you?”

The man looks at me like I’m a pest he quickly wants to squash. “Who the fuck are you?”

“Um...I’m here to kill this piece of shit, and I got here first, so you can just fuck off. The million dollars is mine. Also, I had to fuck the guy to get in here, so there’s no way you’re getting credit. Seriously, you try fucking donkey dick here, and tell me how you like it.”

“Who *are* you?” the man asks, this time sounding perturbed.

I am the newest superhero: Blabi. I have no clue what to do, so I talk until people get tired and walk away.

"Here. Let me give you my card." I reach inside my robe and produce my middle finger. "I'm not giving you my name, you idiot. I'm about to commit murder. Hello…?"

"Are you a friend of Kristoff's?"

Somehow, I feel like this is a test. But what's the right answer? I don't have a clue, so it's wing-it time. "Kristoff doesn't have any friends, but he does have a reputation to maintain. Especially now that he's free and back in the game. Can't let jobs go unfinished." I jerk my head toward Mitch, who's not moving. I'm guessing he's trying to figure out what to do just like I am. One thing is for sure, we'd better do something fast because unless Sam's night watch outside is dead, they're going to spot us through that—

Window. Okay. They saw us.

This is not necessarily a good thing because they're new. If they panic and try to come through the door or take any action besides shooting this guy through the window, Mitch is toast and there isn't a thing I can do about it.

Okay. Think. Think. "Look. You can finish the job if you want. Fine by me. But you'd better talk to the Big K yourself first. He doesn't like anyone getting involved in his business."

"I'm already involved; I hired him."

"You? You hired Kristoff? So you're a Kemmler."

The man frowns, and somehow I know I fucked up. "I know you. You're that woman bodyguard who was all over the news. You took that bullet."

Ugh. My cover is blown.

"Abi, this is Norton Weeno," says Mitch. "The owner and founder of Weeno."

Oh. So that's where the horrible name came from. *Wait. Why's he here?*

"Dammit." Norton shakes his head. "Why couldn't Kristoff finish the job like I asked. Now I have to do it myself and bury two bodies."

"You don't need to do this, Norton," Mitch says, trying his best to remain calm. "You can keep the two million. I'll go grab the contract right now and tear it up."

My mind does a quick sprint through the facts. *Oh! Ohhh…* Mitch is supposed to get a payout at the end of his Weeno contract, and the company is about to go under. *So no more Mitch means no need to pay him.* And with everything that's been playing out in the media, the Kemmlers or Kristoff will get the credit for killing Mitch. Nobody will suspect Weeno.

"It was you all along," I conclude, "wasn't it? You put the hit out on Mitch. You can't afford to pay him because your company is going bankrupt. I'm even guessing you hope to save Weeno with that money."

Norton narrows his eyes. "Shut up."

"I'm right though, aren't I?" I ask.

"I said shut up. Now move next to your boyfriend there."

"I'll do it on one condition, Mr. Weeno; say hello to Mr. Leland Merrick, who's been all over my ass trying to get a scoop." I slide the phone from the pocket of the robe and set it on the kitchen island. "Say hi, Leland. You get all that?"

"Love, I most certainly did." Leland's voice crackles over the little speaker. "One hell of a back scratch, Abi. I'll have the story and these audio files out within the hour. Or…Mr. Norton, you could let these nice people go, and I will give you a head start. I hear Nepal is lovely and doesn't have an extradition treaty with the US. Your other option, of course, is to shoot them in cold blood and spend the rest of your life being someone's Weeno girl. For the record, I'm fine with all the options since I'll get the story."

"Jeez. Thanks, Leland," I say.

"So what's it going to be, Norton?" Mitch asks. "Take whatever money you have and run, or kill us and go to prison?"

"You know, I blame you for Weeno failing," he says to Mitch. "You were supposed to promote our brand, but instead you just made regular men feel inadequate. We had to spend more and more money on those damned inserts because they all wanted to look like you! But could we raise our prices? No."

In the back of my mind, I can hear Leland drooling. More dirt.

"You should've come to me," Mitch says. "We could've worked something out."

"I wanted to. I tried." He begins to cry. "But your army of agents threatened to sue me."

Oh, boo-hoo. "Please put down the gun now, Mr. Weeno, because there are two high-powered rifles pointed at your head, and I'm sure both will hit the target." Words cannot describe how happy I am that the new night-watch guys are well trained. They didn't panic and try to storm the kitchen so the bad guy could be apprehended. We're not the police. We don't worry about arrests or trials. It's about saving the person who's put their life in our hands. Nothing more.

Norton looks up and notices the red dots coming through the window.

"I'd get on the floor if I were you," I say. "They're trained to shoot after ten seconds. Seven, eight, nine, te…"

He does as I ask, and before we know it, Sam's night watch is inside, hog-tying Norton Weeno.

"Wow." Mitch lets out a long breath. "That was intense. I think I wet myself just a little."

"There's a trickle running down my leg as we speak. No joke. Or that could be your baby juice. I'm not sure."

"Guys. Guys!" Leland barks. "I'm still on the phone."

Oops. "If you print that last part, I'll break you, Leland. Goodbye."

"What? No thank-you? No God bless you, Leland, for saving our lives?" he says.

"Thank you. God bless you, Leland. Goodnight." I end the call and look up at Mitch.

"How are you so calm and collected? There's a guy on my kitchen floor who just tried to kill us."

I look over at Sam's crew, who are in the process of securing Norton and calling the police. "Feels like another day at the office to me. Wanna take a shower?"

Mitch shakes his head and laughs. "Can I make us sandwiches first? Stress makes me really hungry."

"Okay. Just don't put anything healthy in mine. I hate vegetables."

"We're going to have to work on your eating habits."

I can think of a lot of other things I'd like to work on, starting with getting to know Mitch better. I know we have insane chemistry. I know we make each other laugh and can talk about anything. I know I'm falling madly in love with him. But what excites me most is getting to know everything about him. He oozes confidence and it's something I've always wanted to have more of. "I think we're going to be really good for each other, Mitch. Really, really good."

CHAPTER TWENTY-TWO

MITCH

Damn, woman, are you trying to give me a heart attack? As I'm gripping Abi by the hips, fucking her from behind with everything I've got, I'm pretty sure she's the one who was meant to be a world-class athlete.

"Harder. Harder." She pants.

I work my thick shaft, aiming for that spot that drives her wild. Don't get me wrong. I love having sex with her, but this is the fourth time tonight. *The Bulge needs his rest.*

"There! There! Right there!" she yells.

Bingo. I lean into her and press the head of my cock until the chain reaction starts. The moan, the orgasmic contractions, her hair whipping back, and...her walls tighten around my cock, giving me just what I want.

I come hard, feeling her muscles milk my shaft for every drop of cum. I can't help growling through every second of it. She makes me feel like an animal, raw and fierce, reduced to nothing but her sex slave.

Abi's smooth skin and soft curves have been replaced by lean muscle since her bootcamp, and I'll take her any way I can get her. It's not every day you find a girl who's this loyal, this protective, this smart and beautiful. We're still getting to know each other, but with each day, I fall more madly in love with her.

Finally, our climaxes subside, and I pull out. *Condom intact. Check!* She's already taking the pill, but after that first little scare, we're not taking any chances. We want to take this time for us before we start thinking of the next step, even if I know we'll get there. I'm already visualizing it. Abi, the most beautiful mother in the world. Me, the best dad ever. Us happy with two incredible little swimmers. Yes, I do mean children. Don't be silly, mate.

I go to the bathroom, clean up, and return to bed, where Abi is tucked under the covers with a dew-covered brow and a content smile on her pink little lips.

I get in next to her and pull her tiny body to my chest. This last week has been crazy with all of the press, the police statements, and the sponsorship offers. No, I'm not going to swim competitively anymore. I'm going to focus on finishing my degree in sports management and helping others reach their goals, but it turns out there are still plenty of companies out there who'd like me to endorse their products. And not just me, but Abi, too. Bullet Buster, the bulletproof vest she wore the night Ash shot her, offered five hundred thousand dollars if she'd be their spokesperson. She nearly wet her trousers when she got the news. Her mom keeps her house, tuition is paid for, and Abi has her money to start that charity she's been talking about. Of course, I'd planned to help her with all of it, but I know she likes paying her own way. She's proud like that.

"Hey, so." She makes tiny circles over my pec. It tickles, but I let her do it anyway. "I was wondering if you're going back to Sydney anytime soon?"

"I was supposed to go for Kristoff's trial, but who knows when that will be. They need to find him first." The good news is I won't have to testify against the Kemmlers. Since Norton Weeno confessed to hiring Kristoff to kill me, there's no real crime to accuse them of. They tried to keep their family's past quiet, but that's not against the law. Now the photos are out and their company is going down the shitter. I almost felt sorry for them until Leland Merrick caught them on a hot mic during their interview, saying they only wished they'd killed me. It would have saved their company.

"Can I come with you when you go?" Abi asks. "I think I'd like to see where you grew up. Meet a few of your friends? Not Ash, though. Already met him. Yuck."

"I only keep in touch with a few people. And the only close family I had was my uncle." I should have spent more time with him when he was alive.

It's one of my biggest regrets. "He was always there—every meet, every practice. He was a good man."

"Sounds like it."

He was the best. "Albert taught me, just like my Grandfather George taught him, that you should never be ashamed of having pride. Pride is what drives ordinary people to do great things." "*Without a deep sense of self and belief that you are meant to win, the only people who would go to war are the tyrants and psychopaths. But thank God for our pride—in our countries, our families, and ourselves. Otherwise, we'd be living in a very different world right now.*" All of the wisdom in our family seemed to be war, history, or ancestor related. To be expected, I suppose, when your grandfather was a World War II photographer and your uncle was in the Special Forces.

"Oh, so he's responsible for that giant ego of yours." Abi laughs. "I wish I could have met your uncle."

"Me too." That's been the hardest part about this past week. Knowing that my uncle will never get to meet her. He would have liked Abi. Her wits, her sassy mouth, her brave heart. But Norton hired Kristoff, and that means the bullet that killed my uncle wasn't about the photos and was probably meant for me. It could have been avoided if Norton had just talked to me. Whatever happens to him, he's got it coming.

"By the way," Abi asks, "what battles was your grandfather in during the war?"

I would tell her everything I know, but maybe it's too early in our relationship to disclose that I am, in fact, a huge history nerd. Have been since I was a kid. Had I not become a swimmer, I likely would have ended up a history professor. I blame my grandfather, who I never met but was a legend in our family and one of the only Australians involved in the infamous Battle of the Bulge. It was the final attempt by the Germans to win the war. The irony is they almost succeeded. The good guys got cocky and underestimated their enemy—a lesson I took with me to every competition. In the end, it was the Allied forces' determination and unwillingness to accept any other outcome besides winning that ended the war.

See. Nerd alert! Yes, I do get the subtle humor of the battle's name, too. Yet another reason I'll wait to tell Abi my dirty nerd-secret. I figure I can let her keep believing I'm a perfect god before dropping the bombshell. *Can't wait to show her the pictures from my pudgy years, too.* She's never going to stop laughing. I looked like a furless baby seal.

"Let's not talk about wars and history right now." I pat her arm.

"Oh, I'm so sorry. I wasn't even thinking about the whole Kemmler thing. Shame what happened to their company. But I told my mom that she should look into making greeting cards. There was a huge shortage for Valentine's Day. I had to go to three different stores to find any, and then I finally decided just to make you one."

Oh crap. "Uh…Valentine's Day wouldn't by chance be today, would it?" I ask.

She narrows her eyes. "Please, please tell me you didn't forget our first Valentine's Day together?"

I hop from the bed and peck her lips. "I'll be right back!" I throw on some clothes, grab my wallet, and bolt from the room. *Flowers. Chocolates. I wonder if they sell cars this late in the day.*

ABI

I smirk as Mitch runs from the room like his pants are on fire. "What a dork." Valentine's Day is tomorrow. Still, that was seriously entertaining. I can't wait to break it to him when he comes back.

My cell rings on the nightstand, and I see it's that Gisselle woman. I hesitate to answer because she either wants something or she's upset because Leland got to break that big story about Weeno.

"Hello?"

"Hey, Abi. Gisselle Walters here."

"What can I do for you?"

"Listen, I need a favor."

I roll my eyes. "It's over. There's no more story to tell."

"Oh, there's always more."

"No."

"What if I told you I know where Kristoff is?"

The hairs on the back of my neck stand straight up. "Is he here? In the US?"

"I'll scratch your back if you scratch mine."

"What is it with you people and your itchy backs?" I let out a breath, mulling it over. Of course I want to know where Kristoff is. He needs to be caught. Not that he's coming after…Mitch…*Oh, god! He totally will!* Mitch is still a witness in his uncle's murder. "What do you want?"

"Leland is trying to find Kristoff, too. I need you to throw him off my trail. I need this interview."

"I'm sorry, but you want to interview this psycho, murdering hit man?" The papers say he's killed over a hundred people. Gisselle is nuts if she's going to run after that man.

"It's the story of a lifetime. Will you help me or not?" she asks.

"Yes! Where is he?" Because my next call will be to Sam. Given his connections in the CIA and FBI, he'll know what to do with the information and keep Kristoff far, far away from us.

"I'll tell you after I get the interview. But in the meantime, I need you to call Leland and say you're worried. Tell him I've run off to Poland. Warsaw. Tell him you're worried because I went alone and you know Kristoff is crazy."

This is Gisselle's big plan? "But won't he get

suspicious? You guys are always trying to throw each other off." I've heard their little fights.

"That's the thing. This time it's the truth. He won't think to look there."

"So…Kristoff is in Warsaw," I say.

"No. Like I said, I'll tell you where he is after I get the interview."

"I'm thoroughly confused. But okay. Just as long as he's not in the US."

"Not yet, but he's coming. Soon."

The call ends, and I resist the urge to panic. I don't even know if I should tell Mitch. He's already been through so much, and I can't stomach seeing him suffer.

No. I can handle this on my own. I'll do as Giselle asks and call Leland and then pass the information to Sam.

The thing is, I'd do anything for Mitch. Just like I'd do anything for my mom, Georgie, and other friends. Protecting those I love is what I'm good at.

I'm actually good at protecting people. Period. It dawns on me that maybe I shouldn't give up being a bodyguard. I can do it part-time while finishing school and continue moonlighting after, when I'm starting my business. *Hmmm…I'll have to give it some thought.* In the meantime…

"Don't worry, Mitchipoo. The dirty hit man will never get near you." I've always got his back. And I know he's got mine.

My phone rings, and I see it's Mitch. "Hello?"

"You're in trouble when I get home, little woman. Today isn't Valentine's Day."

I chuckle. "How'd you find out?"

"Doesn't matter, because now the joke's on you. I felt so guilty for missing it, I was on my way to buy you a Porsche. A big shiny red one."

"Nuh-uh. You big liar." I laugh.

"Guess you'll never know now."

He's messing with me. At least I hope he is. I don't want extravagant gifts. "I'm okay with whatever you give me tomorrow. Especially if it comes in a hot Australian package. Maybe it'll have a bow around a very strategic part I'm super fond of?"

"Is it too soon to say I love you?" His voice isn't playful anymore, and my smile drops away.

"No. It's not."

"Good. Because I plan to say it tomorrow. After I ask you to move in with me."

I can't help tearing up. It's happening so fast, but in my heart, I know it's right. Otherwise, we wouldn't have gone through what we did and come out together on the other side. "Then I plan to say it back and tell you yes, I'd love to live with you."

"What if we say it now?" Mitch is standing in the doorway, looking sexy as hell in a plain white T-shirt and worn jeans, holding his cell.

Every time I see him—those broad shoulders, the beautiful face, those sex-lips—he takes my breath away.

"I could live with that." I stare into his eyes, filled with so much love, and I know that this man might not be alive if it weren't for me, but I wouldn't be living if it weren't for him. "Happy Valentine's Day. I love you, Mitch."

He smiles. "Changed my mind. I'll say it tomorrow. You'll have to wait."

"What?" I crack up, something he makes me do ten times a day. "You're such a dickosaurus."

"Sorry? Don't understand that accent? Did you say you want to see my giant dick?"

"Oh stop. Come over here." He dives into bed and starts kissing my neck. My cell on the nightstand starts vibrating. It's Leland. I know something is up, but it will have to wait. Mitch comes first. Just like I do for him. We're a team now and there's nothing we won't conquer together.

THE END?

Want more OHellNo? Then great! Because, hell yes, it's coming!!

Sign up to my sorta kinda monthly newsletter for updates and alerts. In the meantime, here's a sneak peek of what's coming…

MY PEN IS HUGE
(OHellNo #5)

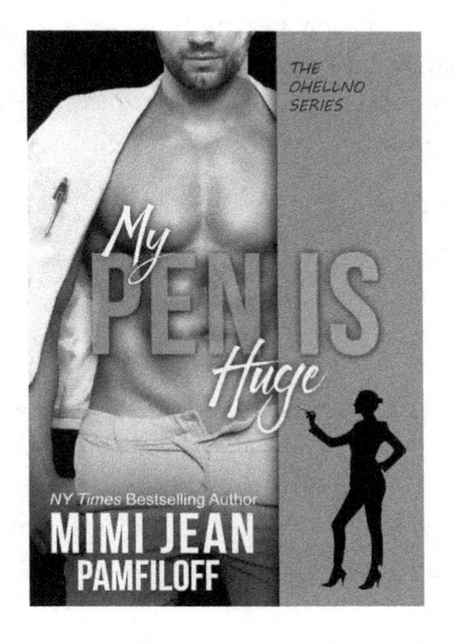

"This is a man's game, love. So step aside."

My name is Leland Merrick and I'm a dedicated journalist—born, raised, and schooled in England. But don't let the nice suits and accent fool you. There isn't a muddy jungle I won't crawl through, a freezing iceberg I won't float on, or a scorching desert I won't cross to get a sensational story. But bloody hell! What was I thinking?

My friend convinced me to take on an intern as a means of getting a free assistant. But this American exchange student I hired, Gisselle, was smart (and not so bad looking) and caught on to my scheme. Little did I know she was watching and learning all my tricks with the intention of becoming a real journalist. Now, everywhere I turn, the little minx is there in her sexy outfits, trying to distract me and steal my stories.

This time, I've got to throw her off my scent because I've come across the big one! The once-in-a-lifetime story people will be talking about for decades.

Besides, who does she think she is? The weight of my pen carries credibility, years of journalistic experience, and a knack for telling a good story. My pen is *huge*. She should take her little play-pen home and give up before I crush her.

AUTHOR'S NOTE

Hello, Mates! I hope this book gave you a little giggle or two. I'm not going to lie, I had a little too much fun investigating all of the slang words for penis. There are hundreds, maybe thousands, each of them funnier than the next. I highly recommend doing an internet search when you need a good chuckle.

As for the next book, *MY PEN IS HUGE*, I'm looking at a fall slot. Be sure you're signed up for my newsletter to get updates and random crap straight from my desk:

Sign up for Mimi's mailing list for giveaways and new release news!

For more frequent fun, STALK me on any of these platforms:

www.mimijean.net
twitter.com/MimiJeanRomance
pinterest.com/mimijeanromance
instagram.com/mimijeanpamfiloff
facebook.com/MimiJeanPamfiloff

And now...what you've been waiting for! FREE SIGNED BULGE BOOKMARKS!

STEP 1: Email me with your shipping address. (Include country if outside the US, *por favor.*)

STEP 2: If you LOVED, LOVED the book and did me the honor of leaving an awesome review, share the link or a screenshot. While supplies last, you'll get a sexy BULGE fridge magnet. (They do go fast, so hurry!) At the very least you'll get a thank-you from me and a tiny unicorn will giggle, creating a rainbow somewhere in the world.

STEP 3: Light a candle in support of my Sharpe so I can complete the harrowing task of signing a thousand bookmarks in one day.

STEP 4: Keep a lookout for a confirmation email from me. (Don't hate me, but sometimes it takes about one month to get to all of them.) If you don't hear from me by then, assume the spam-monster has eaten your email.

All right…back to writing.

Happy Reading Everyone,
Mimi

ACKNOWLEDGMENTS

Another "OH HELL YES!" for Team Mimi, without whom this book #37 couldn't be born! I keep thinking that every time I write a story, I will absolutely have enough time for everything. Inevitably, I end up with my head about to explode because nothing's done and I'm out of time.

So thank you to Dali, Kylie, Latoya, Su, Pauline, and Paul for always being there to get 'er done!

A special thanks to my mate, Sarah Connelly, for helping out with my Aussie slang questions!

To Mack, my new puppy, I kinda hate you right now. That was the biggest puddle EVER you left on my floor. How does a four-pound dog create one gallon of pee?

To my guys, thank you for all of your sacrifices and support. I know it's not easy having a wife/mom who lives in PJs and spends her days in a cave.

With Love,

Mimi

Coming Soon!
COLEL

The Immortal Matchmakers are back!

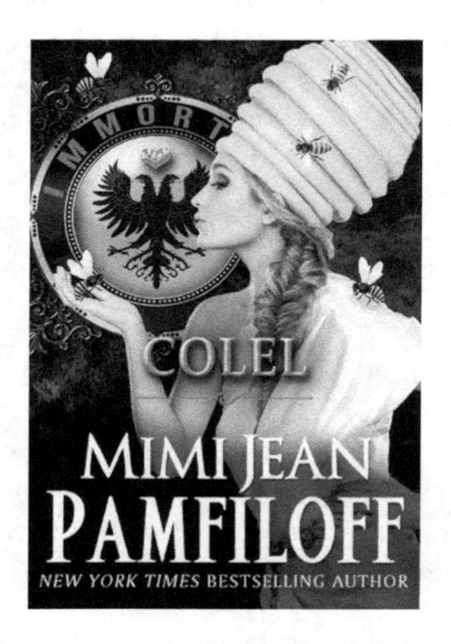

SOMETIMES LOVE BITES AND SOMETIMES IT STINGS.

The Goddess of Bees has been looking for Mr. Right for over seventy thousand years. So when she meets the hunky owner of a local flower shop and explodes with flutters and tingles, she's almost certain that he's the one.

Only two problems: her tiny black-and-yellow army suddenly won't let her anywhere near him, and…is that a freaking epinephrine pen in the fridge? "Dear gods! He's allergic to bees? Say it isn't so."

If simply dating the guy will kill him, how will she ever know for sure if he's really the one?

Colel has a solution, but it's drastic. Like…vampire drastic. And what if he says no?

For More:

www.mimijean.net/colel.html

THE LIBRARIAN'S VAMPIRE ASSISTANT
Book 3 (Standalone)

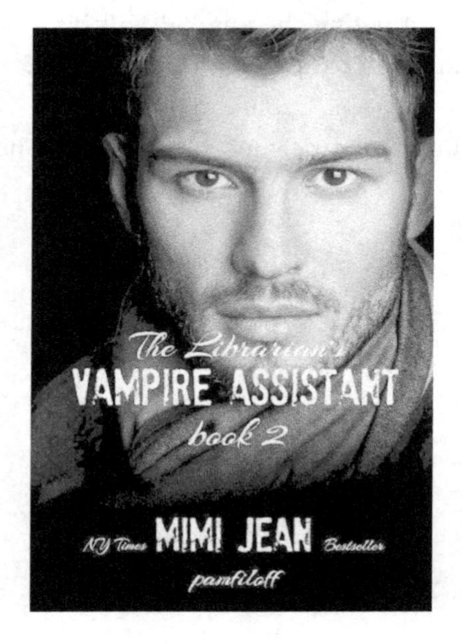

Michael Vanderhorst, the reluctant leader of the vampire world, finds himself caught between protecting the tiny librarian he can't stay away from and solving a mystery that will save the humans.

Coming Fall 2019!

For more, go to:

www.mimijean.net/the-librarians-vampire-assistant-3

MY PEN IS HUGE

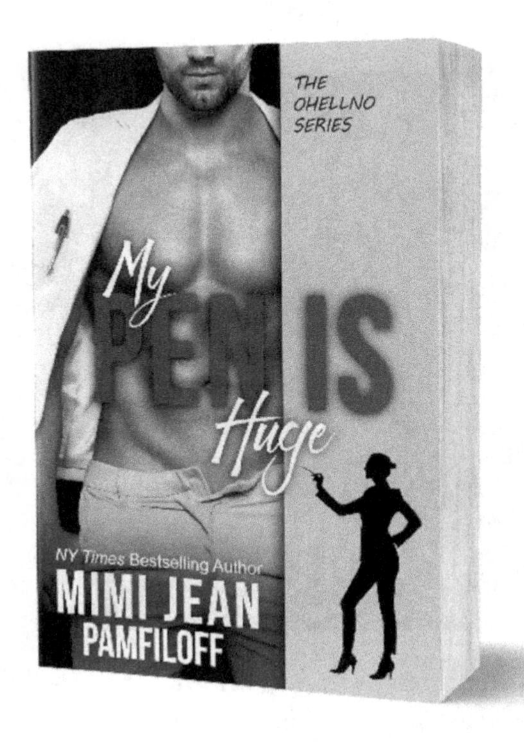

www.mimijean.net/mypen.html

THE BOYFRIEND COLLECTOR
Part Two

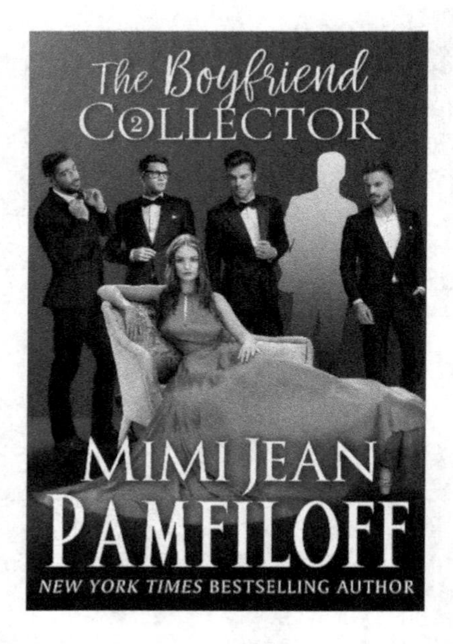

Finally free from the grip of her evil family, will this modern-day Cinderella find her prince?

Don't miss part two of the duet series…

EXCERPT – BOOK ONE
THE BOYFRIEND COLLECTOR

FIND MR. RIGHT IN 30 DAYS?
CHALLENGE ACCEPTED.

Treated like a servant in her own home, twenty-year-old Rose Marie Hale can't stop dreaming of her next birthday. It's the day she'll inherit a fortune, break free from her cruel family, and finally start living her life—finish school, travel, find love. After a lifetime of hardship, it's all she's ever wanted.

But when Rose discovers she must marry before her twenty-first birthday to claim the money, she has no choice but to push herself out into the world in search of a man she can love and trust. Unfortunately, those are the very things that have been used as weapons against her.

With only a month to go, can she find true love? Or will her past hold her back, leaving her penniless and alone?

(Part One of Two)

CHAPTER ONE

BEX

Well, this is not a promising start. Seated in my black leather armchair, I rub the stubble on my jaw and glance down at the questionnaire in my other hand. The agitated young woman lying on the couch in front of me has left the entire form blank except for her name at the top. Rose Marie Hale.

Rose. The name fits her. At first glance she looks like a delicate, fragrant flower—long, lean stems for legs, trim body, and blonde silky hair—but a sharpness in her dark brown eyes tells me she's not all soft petals.

I make a quick note of my observation in the margin of the page before interrupting her fast talking—something about dating…or men…or I'm unsure, actually. "Miss Hale, excuse my insensitivity, but I'm here to help people, not waste their time. Or mine. So what, exactly, do you mean when you say you have to find a husband? Sounds like you need a friend or a dating app, not therapy." I rest my gold pen across the clipboard on my lap, waiting for her to answer.

Like the pen, this office—situated in a renovated brick warehouse in Atlanta's trendy Buckhead district—once belonged to my father, who was also a psychologist. I stepped in, merging my practice with his when he became ill last spring. By the time he died a month ago, I learned many things about the man, bad things I loathe him for. The first disappointment came when I discovered he never practiced what he preached in terms of treating his patients, who were receiving little more than touchy-feely pep talks: *You can do it. I believe in you.*

Complete bullshit. The only thing he accomplished was creating a steady stream of customers who became dependent on him instead of themselves.

I don't blow smoke up patients' asses just so they'll come back next week for another fix of self-esteem injections. I say it like it is, and if they truly want to get their lives together, they listen.

As for this woman on my couch, I don't know what to make of her other than the obvious that she's in her early twenties, her attractiveness is distracting, and I'm unsure why the hell she's here. If she's looking for boyfriend advice, she's come to the wrong place.

"Dr. Hughes? Are you listening?" she says, her slender body stretched across my white couch.

Not really. Her lips are moving so fast, I feel like I'm at an auction. "Rose Marie—"

"I prefer Rose. Just Rose," she corrects.

"Okay. *Rose*, I'm sorry, but I'm a psychologist, not a romance coach."

She sits up and plants her feet on the floor. Her red heels look expensive, as does the matching red sweater. Her jeans are the type most men like on women—tight, a bit short to show off some toned calf, and cut to accentuate the feminine curve of her hips.

"I'm not here for love coaching," she says with a frantic tone. "I have to get married. Quickly. My entire life depends on it."

Trying to hide my impatience, I lift my brows. She strikes me as the quintessential entitled princess who thinks her social life is the most important thing on the planet. *Oh no, someone didn't like my selfie on Instagram. Whatever shall I do?* If she can't give me a legitimate reason to see her or convince me that she's here to work, I'll turn her away.

"This isn't the Dark Ages," I say. "Many women lead long happy lives and never marry."

"I know. And that's not what this is about. Not even close."

"All right." I inhale slowly, taking a moment to rally my patience. "Why don't you try explaining it once more."

She lies back down, crossing her long legs at the ankles, her large eyes focused on the exposed wooden beam running across the ceiling.

I wait while she mulls. She's hopefully realizing

how silly it is to pay a licensed therapist, with a doctorate in social neuroscience, just to talk about boys. I never would have agreed to see her if I knew this was her "problem," but Rose left a frantic message with my service last night. A short conversation followed, where she disclosed nothing and pleaded to see me first thing this morning.

Fast-forward to fifteen minutes ago. I get to my office before my assistant has arrived and find Rose walking around the hallway. My office is one of many on the second floor, so it's easy to miss. Downstairs are several boutiques and a small coffee shop, where I practically live between patients.

Which reminds me that I skipped the latte this morning, and I'm wishing I hadn't because I'll need a heavy dose of caffeine to keep up with all the whining I'm hearing.

Yes, if I were a lesser man, I might be content to sit here all day, staring at a gorgeous woman while she rambles on about her love life. But I am *not* that man. I'm here to help people. *And I think this woman came to the wrong place.*

Rose

I knew it would be a waste of time coming here, but this exceeds my worst expectations. Everything about this guy says he doesn't care. The drab gray tie, plain white dress shirt, and black slacks tell me he doesn't have a warm bone in his body. All business. The polished concrete floor and a bland gray rug to accent his work space confirm he lacks imagination. And not one item in his office indicates he has any hobbies or passions. I don't even see a family photo despite the fact he's fidgeting with his wedding ring. *Married.* But he obviously doesn't want to think about her at work. What does that say about him?

"Rose," he says in a deep, authoritative voice that sounds rehearsed, "this session is only an hour, and I get paid either way."

In other words, I should start talking if I want my money's worth. But Dr. Bexley Hughes doesn't seem interested in hearing anything I have to say. I doubt I'd be sitting here at all if I hadn't begged him last night over the phone. But I need help, and now that his father is dead, I have no one else to turn to.

I squirm on his lumpy couch. The fabric is soft—some sort of white velveteen—but the springs are pushing into my ass. *Another bad sign.* He doesn't care about his patients enough to buy comfortable furniture.

I get up and walk over to the wall of books behind the black leather armchair where he's seated. I know he's waiting for me to explain why I need to get married, but his intense stare makes it difficult. I don't like it or him one little bit.

Ironically, if I saw him walking down the street, the two of us complete strangers, he'd have me looking twice. Dark hair, light blue eyes, and a hard jawline. Classically handsome. Just my type. Though he's a little older, maybe twenty-nine or thirty.

Of course, all that's irrelevant. Doesn't matter if he's good looking. Doesn't matter if I like his personality. The question is, will Dr. Bexley Hughes help me? He seems more uncaring and heartless than my family, if that's even possible.

With our backs to each other, I pluck a book off the shelf and thumb through the crisp white pages. It's inscribed to Dr. Murdoc Hughes, his late father. *Funny, they look nothing alike.* Murdoc had warm brown eyes and an even warmer smile.

"I met your dad before he died." I turn and speak to the back of Bexley Hughes's head. "He was a good man. Maybe the only decent person I've ever met. I hoped you'd be like him. Are you?"

"You knew my father?" he says with a tinge of skepticism, pivoting in his seat to face me.

I nod.

"But you were never a patient."

"No," I confirm. "He told me to see *you* if I changed my mind."

"Changed it about what?"

I shut the book with a clap, place it back on the shelf, and walk over to the white couch, where I sit with hands clasped. I don't know why *this* Dr. Hughes makes me so uneasy, but he does. It's odd given how I'm no stranger to unpleasant people.

"I met your father last spring," I say, "when he gave a lecture at my university about the psychology of storytelling. I am—I mean, I *was* an English major. I dropped out." I had promised myself that no matter what my grandmother did or said, I wouldn't leave school this time. But she has a way of slithering inside my head and undermining every positive thought, every productive intention—"*You should be home, Rose, fulfilling the promise to your dead mother. There will be time for college later.*" After weeks of being guilted, I finally gave in. *Idiot.*

Or maybe it was fate?

Had I not stopped taking classes, I never would've been home on that fateful day when I overheard a strange conversation my grandmother had with her lawyer. Then I wouldn't have had that quiet nagging feeling in the back of my mind, telling me that maybe, just maybe there was more to my mother's will. And I certainly wouldn't have been prompted to go through my grandmother's safe a week ago when she left it open by accident.

But now I know the horrible truth: The copy of the will shown to me all those years ago was a fake, and everything I've been promised is about to be taken away.

I continue, "I liked your father's perspective about how every epic story has a villain, a victim, and a knight." The older Dr. Hughes said that in the world of psychology, a therapist's job is to make every patient their own knight, the hero of their story. "When I decided I needed to talk to someone, I looked him up. He called me back right away, and it was the first time I remembered anyone just listening and wanting to help. Nothing in return."

I was really sorry when I found out he was ill, but he urged me to come in and see his son instead. Trusting strangers isn't easy for me, so I told him I'd think about it. Of course, the situation I'm facing now is entirely different. It's no longer about the guilt or the shame my family has poisoned me with. This is about justice. This is about wrong versus right.

I look away from the younger Dr. Hughes's judgmental gaze and add, "Your dad told me if I ever needed someone to trust, someone who'd help me, it would be you."

I suddenly notice Dr. Hughes's face is a hostile shade of red, and while I didn't think it possible for anyone to look more anal retentive and intimidating, he's just proven me wrong.

He sets his clipboard on top of a little wooden table to his side and leans forward. "I think it's time for you to go."

I blink. "Sorry?"

"I can't help you."

"Did I miss something?" He's clearly pissed, but what did I do?

"I am not the right therapist for you, Miss Hale, but I can suggest a colleague who specializes in relationships and commitment issues."

I frown. "Why would I need help with that?" All right, yes, I have issues in those areas, but not how he thinks.

"Didn't you say you're here because you're trying to find a husband?"

"Yes, but—"

"But then I'm *not* the doctor for you," he cuts me off.

The anger percolates in my stomach. I'm done with being dismissed, and I won't tolerate being treated like I'm worthless. *Not anymore.*

"You said you're here to help people," I argue. "Well, here I am, needing help."

He stands, walks to the door, and opens it. The expression on his face turns from anger to simple disgust.

What kind of therapist just shuts a person down like this? It's humiliating, and with all I've been through, I'm not game for his special breed of head trip. He has no clue what's at stake and the mental torture I've survived.

Doesn't matter. He's right. He can't help me. I stand and walk to the door, stopping in front of him. I'm five seven, but he's much taller, so I tilt my head back to look him in the eye. There is no compassion to be found in their soft blue hues. Just ice. "I don't know what I said to piss you off, but you've got the wrong impression about why I came here. I'm just trying to survive."

"Aren't we all." He jerks his head toward the

doorway as if to say *get the fuck out.*

This man doesn't just have a stick up his ass, it's an entire forest. "You're nothing like your father. You're not even half the man he was."

"Thank God for small favors," he replies.

I sail out, wondering what he means, and the door slams behind me.

Heartless bastard. He couldn't just hear me out?

Suddenly, I realize how alone I truly am. I stop in the hallway and cover my face with my hands, fighting off an imminent meltdown. I hate to cry. It makes me feel weak, and I don't want to be weak anymore. But I don't know what I'm going to do. The clock is ticking, and right now, the whole world is against me. Not hyperbole. Not a joke. Everyone I've ever known is against me, and I need at least one—just one goddamned person to trust.

ABOUT THE AUTHOR

MIMI JEAN PAMFILOFF is a *New York Times* bestselling author who's sold over one million books around the world. Although she obtained her MBA and worked for more than fifteen years in the corporate world, she believes that it's never too late to come out of the romance closet and follow your dreams.

Mimi lives with her Latin lover hubby, two pirates-in-training (their boys), and their three spunky dragons (really, just very tiny dogs with big attitudes) Snowy, Mini, and Mack, in the vampire-unfriendly state of Arizona.

She hopes to make you laugh when you need it most and continues to pray daily that leather pants will make a big comeback for men.

Sign up for Mimi's mailing list for giveaways and new release news!

STALK MIMI:

www.mimijean.net
twitter.com/MimiJeanRomance
pinterest.com/mimijeanromance
instagram.com/mimijeanpamfiloff
facebook.com/MimiJeanPamfiloff

CPSIA information can be obtained
at www.ICGtesting.com
Printed in the USA
LVHW032100061219
639738LV00005B/372/P